FOREVER

BOOK ONE IN THE FOREVER SERIES

MARY A. WASOWSKI

Copyright © 2014 by Mary A. Wasowski
Cover Design by Okay Creations

Printed in the United States of America
First Edition: February 2014
Library of Congress Cataloging-in-Publication Data

http://authormaryawasowski.com/

Wasowski, Mary A.
    Forever (*Book One in The Forever Series*)/Mary A. Wasowski – 1st ed
    ISBN-13: 978-0989623834

    1. Forever—Fiction.   2.   Fiction—Romance
    3. Fiction—Contemporary Romance

For my family.
You help me make the impossible become the possible.
I love you with all my heart.

Part One
Reese

CHAPTER ONE

A new beginning...

LOOKING AROUND MY now empty bedroom, I wondered how had the last ten years of my life spent here been reduced to packed boxes? The last three years had been spent living away at college. I always looked forward to coming home to the comforts of this room and all of the memories it held for me. As I labeled my last box and pushed it in the corner, I closed my eyes as the memories came crashing back to me.

This is the room that my Nana made up for me when I had to come live with her and my Granddaddy. She filled it with my personal things, like new books to read and stuffed animals to snuggle with when I was scared of the thunderstorms. We said our prayers here in this room every night and looked up to the heavens to mom and dad, knowing they were looking down on us.

It wasn't supposed to be this way. My parents should be here seeing me off, begging me not to go, but they're gone. All I had were memories of our short time together. I was ten years old when daddy died. He was crossing the street and out of nowhere a passing truck driver mowed him down… and left him for dead. As my father struggled to cling to life, my family had been enjoying a day by the lake waiting for him to arrive. I remember laughing and Granddaddy splashing me with water. My mom and Nana were busy preparing lunch while I laughed and played.

Hours had gone by, and with no sign of daddy, we went home. We were unpacking the car back at Nana's house when we were greeted by the local sheriff and his deputy. Pottersville was a small town where all your neighbors knew each other. I loved this town when I was little. Naturally, I never could imagine myself leaving it. Sheriff Danforth asked if he could speak with my mom and grandparents. I stayed outside and played with Bubba, Granddaddy's golden retriever. My smiles turned to cries as I heard my mom scream from the house. I ran to her, but Nana held me back. Granddaddy was holding Mom in his arms, just rocking her as if she were a baby again, shushing her, and urging her to breathe. "Please breathe, baby, we will get through this...please," over and over again he whispered to her.

Two days later, I watched my father get lowered down into the ground. We were told that my father had died en route to the hospital, where he was pronounced D.O.A. The injuries that he sustained were too severe, and there was nothing they could have done to save him. The truck driver was caught the next day and taken into custody for driving under the influence. He only spent seven months in jail, a small price to pay for his act of carelessness. According to the law, he paid his debt to society, but not to our family. He *killed* my father and destroyed my world. The anniversary of my father's death delivered another devastating blow to our family. My mother never was the same after losing her beloved Daniel. She left me a letter telling me to be a good girl for Nana and Granddaddy. She said she was sorry that she had to leave me, and as much as she loved me, she just wasn't strong enough to go on without my father by her side. She begged me to forgive her for her weakness, to remember that I was loved very much, and one day we would all be together again. I could feel her heartache in her written words.

Together again? Her words burned me like touching the flames in a fire. How could my mother believe that I would be okay without her; that I would not be as broken hearted as she was? HOW DARE SHE? Mama was right about one thing, she was weak! I vowed never to become a person like the one she had become. I would grow up and be strong. I was going to make something out of my life! I thanked God every day for my grandparents who put their own personal grieving aside to take care of me and to make sure I was okay first. Again, I looked to my empty room and shook my head at the fact that I wouldn't be living here anymore.

"No! I'm not going. I'll finish school here and find a job." Not realizing I said that out loud, my grandmother Lila was standing behind me laughing. *Why was she laughing? Doesn't she know how much I am going to miss her?*

"Nana! Stop laughing at me."

"Oh, my beautiful girl, come here and sit with me for a minute. I'm not laughing at you, so calm yourself. Maybe I was laughing because you make me so happy."

"How blessed I have been to have you as my granddaughter and to know I have had a hand in the strong woman you have become."

"How do you do it?"

"Do what, honey?"

Now wrapped in my Nana's arms, I said, "Make me feel better."

"It's my job to know these things. You have been my shining light since the day you screamed yourself into this crazy world. I have not regretted one day spent with you. As hard as it is to move on, you just have to, honey."

"Why did she do it, Nana? Losing daddy was hard enough, but to lose both my parents within a year of each other? It's just *so* cruel."

"I know it is, honey, and sometimes we are faced with things in this life that we are not meant to understand. Everything does happen for a reason, and hopefully, one day we will get the answers we need. For now… the best thing for you to do is to go out and live your life. Now, enough of this wallowing in the past, your Freddy Macaroons is waiting on you."

"Nana! His name is Freddy Mac, and although he loves your cookies, he doesn't want you to share the nickname you have for him with anyone." I laughed for a few minutes after Nana mentioned the nickname that she gave my best friend. Freddy Mac, a.k.a. Freddy Mackelstein, was born and raised in the Bronx. He moved to Georgia for his father's job and attended Georgia State University, where we met on orientation day. I'll never forget watching Freddy from across the campus. He looked completely frazzled and lost. My southern manners did not escape me. I walked over to help him. I had visited the campus on several occasions, so I already knew the campus well enough.

His head was buried in his hands, I softly cleared my throat to get his attention. Freddy looked up after hearing me. "Hi there, my name is Reese. You look a bit…lost. Can I help you find your way?"

"Have the gods answered my prayers and sent me an angel? If you are that angel, then, yes, please help me!" After hearing that very cheesy line, I thought helping this stranger didn't seem like a good idea after all. Then he smiled and broke out into laughter. I guess the look on my face said it all for him. "Sorry, I didn't mean to freak you out. Please help me navigate my way around here. If you prove to be successful with your tour guide skills, then you are hired as my new best friend."

"Apology accepted, but before I accept your job offer, I will need to know who I'm working for." I couldn't help but smile and laugh. He was adorable.

"Mac, Freddy Mac, really Mackelstein but don't tell anyone. And you are…Reese?"

"Mitchell, Reese Mitchell. Pleasure to meet you, Freddy. So, you look a bit lost. What can I do?"

Sighing…"I don't know how a handsome New York Jewish boy ended up here, shvitzing in this god awful heat. But yes, I'm lost and need help." Spending the entire day with Freddy calmed my own fears of beginning college. We were thick as thieves for the first two years at Georgia State University. He became a permanent fixture at

4

my side, and anytime I would go home to Pottersville to visit my grandparents he was with me. Always my protector to ward off the jerk-off guys that would constantly hit on me at parties, Freddy wasn't intimidating by any means, but he sure could talk his way out of any situation. I was sad when he told me he decided to transfer to NYU after completing our second year, but New York had everything he wanted and it was his home. I stayed behind and continued on without my best friend. Then, I received an opportunity to model.

I was part of the drama club on campus and acted in some plays. One night after my performance, I was approached along with some other girls to model for some local designers participating in a charity event. After talking it over with my grandparents, I decided to go for it and see where it could lead me. Freddy gasped excitedly into the phone after I called him about it. The designers loved me for my height, and they seemed to be happy with my looks. I never really paid too much attention to my figure, but I was naturally thin and blessed with curves in the right places. Nana never liked me doing too much change to my hair, so I always left it in its natural brown color and kept it long. As time went on, the stylists gave me a more modern long style.

Things couldn't have been going better for me. I was maintaining my 4.0 GPA and earning a steady paycheck because of the modeling jobs. Everything was great until Freddy had sent me a link to a website he found me on. I was horrified with what I saw. It was my face, but it wasn't me. *I was watching myself in a porn movie. Oh my god!* How was I going to explain this to my grandparents? Or the very small town I come from? It turned out that one of the photographers who was a last minute add-on, filmed me and some others while we were working. He used our images for the filth that he called art.

I had no choice but to be honest and tell my grandparents right away. We hired a lawyer, and he was able to get the movie taken down from the sites that it was featured on. He immediately filed a lawsuit against the photographer and the well-known firm he worked for. We stopped further production of the film, and we won our case. Needless to say, my junior year was not as amazing as I thought it was going to be. No matter where I was on campus, I felt like a bright spotlight was shining on me for the world to see. Girls would talk behind my back, and guys would try to grab my ass or whistle rude catcalls at me. Nana always used to say that people find it easier to believe the bad than the good. I knew who I was. What happened to me was not my fault, and only the people closest to me truly believed that.

Eventually the chatter calmed down, and I felt I could show my face again back home. I couldn't wait to pack up my dorm room, go back home, and hide from the big bad world. Knowing Nana, she was having none of that! I was to finish with my last term of my junior year, and then come home like everyone else. Never disobeying her, I did what she asked of me. Sure enough, they showed up with their U-Haul and picked me up as promised. It was comforting to return home to Pottersville.

What Nana didn't know was that I was thinking of transferring out of GSU and taking Freddy up on his offer to move in with him in New York. I secretly sent my admission papers to NYU as a joke, never believing that I would get in, but I did. Now I just had to tell the grandparents. Over dinner, I broke the news. Surprisingly, they were happy for me. They both gave me their blessing. Nana was never one to dwell in the past, and she wanted more for me. So after many hugs, I called Freddy and told him that I would see him in August.

My final summer with Nana and Granddaddy seemed to go by so quickly. I tried to spend as much time with them as I could. As much as I didn't want to leave them, I was so excited to start my new life in New York.

"Hey, you two, if the crying and the hugging has ceased, my granddaughter has a plane to catch."

"Oh Granddaddy, we still have time."

"No you don't, sweetheart. You and your Nana have been talking up in here for two hours already." *Wow! I guess I shouldn't be surprised; talking to Nana is effortless, and it's very easy to shut the rest of the world out.*

"Granddaddy, am I doing the right thing?" I looked into his green eyes, and waited for him to tell me no, but that's not what he said. He took me in his arms, hugged me tightly, and kissed the top of my head.

"Sweetheart, you were meant for bigger things than this small town. You go to New York and make your dreams come true". He gave me one last hug before Nana came over to give me a few more of her amazing words of wisdom.

"Now, my sweet girl, you listen to your Granddaddy and be happy. You never know what sweet gifts life is going to give you. You may even find your future husband in the big city and live happily ever after." With one more hug and kiss from the two of them, I was shoved into the backseat of my cab, and they waved me off. I cried the entire time to the airport. I knew I was leaving my past behind that included losing my parents, the modeling nightmare, and the sadness that I tried very hard to keep at bay. I would miss my grandparents so much, but seeing me earn my college degree and just being happy was all they wanted. How could I let them down after all they had done for me?

CHAPTER TWO

Small fish in a big pond...

THE FLIGHT TO New York was smooth. I slept for most of it, only waking up to stow my tray table back in its place. Arriving twenty minutes ahead of schedule allowed me some time to freshen up and grab a coffee. It was only eight a.m. and I knew Freddy was probably still at home asleep. Granddaddy had arranged for a car to pick me up and take me to Freddy's apartment in Washington Square. Freddy's uncle had owned an apartment that he usually sublet to students, but since Freddy was back living in the city, his parents arranged for him to live there. The idea of me becoming his roommate came later when Granddaddy decided it would be better for me to live with someone I knew and trusted, than a complete stranger.

Hitting the buzzer several times and getting no response, I was beginning to get annoyed when Freddy screamed out from the top window. "It's about time my Georgia peach arrived." Yeah…I was embarrassed since I was now surrounded by on-lookers curious to why the guy above was screaming and calling me a peach. My face turned five shades of red while waiting for Freddy to drag his ass down and welcome me to my new home for the next year.

"Oh, I missed you so much! Come here, you."

I couldn't resist his charm and gave him the biggest hug I could manage. "I missed you too, and thank you for the…welcome."

"My pleasure, love, now let's get you settled. As you can see Bernie and Barbara spared no expense. Your room has a fresh coat of paint, and get this…new bed linens. Holy shit! You got a new blankie of your very own."

"Will you stop it? I like your mom and dad, they are so sweet, and all you do is mock on them. Why do you do that, Freddy?"

"Oh come on, Peaches. I'm their only son, and one day I will probably be wiping their asses when they are really old. I might as well get my jabs in now when they can still comprehend what I'm teasing them about."

"You are so bad, but I guess if they don't seem to mind your humor, who am I to judge?"

My boxes had arrived a few days before, and Freddy, the prince that he is, unpacked all my things and began setting up my room. I didn't send much to New York; the majority of my personal belongings were back home with Nana. I only needed a few mementos to make my room a home. Freddy placed all my favorite pictures on the mantel in the living room along with his, and he placed a few in my room. The only picture that brings me comfort is the one of me and my parents taken a week before my dad's death. We were in the orchard picking peaches, and Nana snapped our picture. The other one I hold dear is one of my grandparents sitting on their porch swing. They are so much in love after so many years together. Nana predicted I may meet my future husband here in New York, but I wasn't holding my breath.

My first week in New York was all about getting settled into my new apartment and learning my way around the new neighborhood. Freddy showed me where the grocery store was, corner deli, and of course, all the Starbucks surrounding our apartment. Freddy only had a few months until he would graduate in December. He attended three summers of classes and never had taken a single vacation during that time. He wanted to get his degree so he could start his career, which he had done months before I arrived. His parents knew fashion was his calling, but they wanted him to earn his business degree first. If he was going to be the master in charge of his own company one day, then he would need to know how to run it.

Freddy had interned for Ralph Lauren and then was hired as a junior designer to work along with the creative teams that were in charge of Fashion Week. *Oh my goodness! Fashion week!* I shrieked with giddiness when I heard that. Freddy had passed along my portfolio along with some new pictures that I had taken before leaving Georgia. I wasn't sure that I wanted to continue modeling, but Freddy quickly changed my mind.

One afternoon, I was introduced to a woman named Marsha Malin, who later would become my agent and dear friend. She was very impressed with my portfolio. She offered me a spot modeling for three designers and a new upcoming superstar, who I proudly call my best friend. After we worked out the details, Marsha suggested we get out of the office and grab lunch at her favorite deli. "You won't find sandwiches like this in Georgia… only in New York."

"Aren't you supposed to tell me I shouldn't be eating this stuff, and stick with salads?" I smiled at her as she grinned back at me.

"First of all, I'm not one of those agents who will starve you. Reese, you are beautiful just the way you are, and we see something in you that the other girls simply do not possess."

"What's that? I'm just a girl from a small town in the south. What makes me so different from the other girls?" *My self-doubt was rearing its ugly head, and I began to think about the dirty pictures and the video taken of me and the other models.* It was time to come clean with her about my past and what had happened back home in Georgia.

"Marsha, I need to tell you something before we go any further." I watched Marsha place her menu down and lean towards the table looking directly into my eyes.

"Reese, don't plotz on me, okay?" *Plotz? What does that mean? That's a new word I haven't heard before.* "I already know what happened in Georgia with that putz of a photographer. No worries, sweetheart. We do a thorough background check on all of our girls that we hire. Freddy filled us in on the rest. Believe me when I say this, you will always encounter a putz in this business, but that one… he will never be able to land a credible job again."

"I'm so sorry you ever had to know that about me. I'm incredibly embarrassed by it all, and I just fear that it will follow me everywhere I go."

"It may, Reese, but we're hiring you anyway. So again, no worries. I'm hungry, let's eat already."

"Marsha, can I ask you a question, and then I promise we can order?" She drops the menu again. "What does plotz mean?" My very loud agent began to roar in laughter when I asked her my question. I asked her again, and tried to quiet her at the same time.

"I'm sorry, honey; I guess I need to let you in on all my slang words I like to use. I just thought with Freddy being your friend, you would know them all already."

"You would be surprised how my friend can still shock me."

"Well, plotz means don't have a stroke, or calm down. My mother used to say it all the time to my father, and to her father before that. I guess it's one of the good ones that stuck with me all these years." Satisfied with her answer, Marsha signaled the waiter over, and we ordered the biggest pastrami and swiss sandwiches I have ever seen. Of course, I couldn't finish mine, but I brought the rest home for Freddy to enjoy.

I heard things can happen in a New York minute. Well that was certainly true in my case. My first few weeks living there had been quite the adventure. Living with Freddy was so much fun. I never realized how much I had missed him until we were reunited and now living together as roommates. He was so busy with his work, and today was my first day of classes. Freddy started the next day for what would be his last few classes of his college career. He had taken the day off to follow me around today. I tried to talk him out of it, but he wanted to make sure I found my way without any issues.

My first class was Psychology One, an introductory class that was pretty basic. Freddy and I walked in and grabbed two seats at the top. I was always one to sit in the first row, afraid that I would miss something. I never had any problems making my grades. Freddy was whispering something in my ear when I noticed… *Him. Gasp!* My eyes focused in on the very good looking guy that just walked in to the expansive room. He was tall, probably around six feet or so, he had brown hair, and I could see his tight stomach through his t-shirt. *Get a grip!* Unsure of what was coming over me, I quickly turned to Freddy before the handsome stranger caught me staring.

"Hey, what's got your panties in a twist, Peaches? Or should I say…*who?*"

"Freddy! Keep your voice down." I lowered myself down in my seat to not draw attention to myself. Freddy tended to be on the loud side, and after his comment, some of the other students turned to look at us. I was about to say something to him when my attention was once again focused on the hot guy now talking to my professor. They were in a short conversation, and then the hot guy grabbed his backpack and walked out. The professor shut the door rather loudly to get our attention, and class had begun.

"So are you going to answer my question?"

I turned to Freddy as we make our way to the library after class. "What question?" I asked him.

"Oh, you know, Peaches. The hot guy that had your attention before your very boring class began."

"Okay, you're right. I was staring at him. I don't know what it is, but something about him caught my interest."

"Well, I would have thought by the look on your face that you definitely wanted to tap that. I'm sure you got some practice in before coming up to the big city." Freddy was laughing at this point, but his comments stopped me dead in my tracks. I felt my blood heating with anger at my best friend.

Freddy didn't realize that I wasn't even by his side anymore, until he turned around to watch me walk in the other direction. He called out to me, but I ignored him until he caught up and pulled me back to him. "Hey, what's wrong, Peaches? Talk to me, please?"

"Let go of my arm, Freddy. And if you really have to ask… then you are dumb as bricks."

"I guess I do have to ask, because I don't know what the hell has gotten into you."

"Your rude comment is what has gotten into me. How could you say that to me after what I went through? So because pictures of me circulated around that implied I was a porn star, then of course I would be a whore who sleeps around, too!"

"Oh my god, that's not what I meant at all, Reese. How could you think that?"

"I think that because that's how it sounded, Freddy. I dealt with the whispers behind my back, the mean girls, and fighting off the advances of guys that just wanted to fuck me because they thought I would easily give it up. My last year at GSU was hell, so forgive me for being a bit defensive."

"I'm sorry, Peaches. You know I would never hurt you. I was only kidding, and now I realize it was bad taste on my part. Honestly, I didn't mean anything by it. Please say that you forgive me?" I looked into my best friend's eyes to see him now crying. My heart broke, and I immediately wrapped my arms around him.

"I'm sorry too, Freddy. My wounds are still wide open and filled with hurt. I'm just trying to move forward and start fresh. I want to forget everything that happened in Georgia." *I wasn't just talking about the modeling mishap; I was remembering my parents' deaths, and all the pain that I have carried with me since they left me.*

"Reese, what happened to you was not your fault! Your grandparents stopped it before it ever got out of hand. You need to let that part of your life go and not worry about it anymore."

"Freddy, don't you get it? Pictures are forever. This will follow me everywhere I go. I might as well staple this to every job application I apply for. Can you imagine if this ever got out, or years from now when I'm a teacher? I would be fired, and no parent would want me teaching their children."

"Stop it now, Reese! You are amazing, beautiful, and very smart. You are going to be an awesome teacher, so stop worrying about it. And hopefully you hook up with that hot guy from your psychology class! Maybe that will relax you."

"You know I'm still a virgin, right?" Now it was Freddy's turn to turn five shades of red. Who knew that I could embarrass him with my sexual status?

CHAPTER THREE

Hello Stranger...

FREDDY AND I talked all night after my blow-up. He was very open with me about his conquests with men. Basically he told me everything and anything. He was never embarrassed about coming out... not even to his parents. Freddy, from a young age, never felt "normal," something was different. When he figured out he was gay, he came out. He made his declaration on his seventeenth birthday; his father had a hard time at first accepting that his only son was gay. His mother was more understanding, but ultimately sided with his father, until Freddy gave them an ultimatum. He loved his parents, but refused to live his life in secret or be blamed for shaming his family. His parents decided that they loved their son more than risking losing him altogether.

My virginity was intact at twenty years old. I guess I never was in a hurry to trade in my V-card. I had my share of opportunities with a few boyfriends that I had back home, but I never really felt a deep connection with anyone. I always said no. Having been raised in the Bible Belt of the country did not make me a prude, but again, a woman's virginity is sacred. So I was waiting for the right person that I could give not only my body to, but also my heart.

One week to the day after my first fight with Freddy had passed.

I never did make it to the library, so that was my first stop before my morning classes. I grabbed a coffee and sat down to peruse some of the material I needed to know for my test that I would be taking that day when my eyes met his... the handsome stranger from psychology class. He was watching me, and all of the sudden, I was shy. I smiled to myself and looked down to my book. He sat down right at my table, but said nothing. He was breathtakingly gorgeous. *I'm sitting here in silence, but he's not saying anything either.* I look up to him through my glasses, and I let out a quiet laugh. He glanced back at me with his beautiful sexy smile, and suddenly got up to leave. I couldn't help but let out a louder laugh.

Was the handsome stranger shy as well? Who knew if I would ever see him again, but if I did, I would make sure to actually move my lips and use my voice.

I was worn out from my course load already. I gave up stressing over how I did on my first psych test. I needed coffee if I was going to keep my eyes open for that night's studying. Walking over to the coffee station, I was nearly knocked over by someone not looking where he's going. I dropped my books only to look up into the eyes of the handsome stranger. He crouched down to help me, and our eyes locked on one another.

"Hi, I'm Reese Mitchell. Um…Thank you for your help."

"It's no bother at all. I'm Walker Reed."

Now that the handsome stranger had a name, we could easily talk to one another. "I've seen you at the library, and I thought you were in my psychology class, but I only saw you once."

"You certainly have a detailed memory, Reese. Yes, I was in psychology, but I would have never dropped that class had I known you were in it. How foolish of me."

"Well, Walker, pleasure to meet you. As much as I would like to continue chatting, I need to get home. May I have my books back please?"

"I will give you your books back, but on one condition. Please join me for dinner on Friday night."

"That sounds lovely, but Friday is not good for me."

"What about Saturday? We don't have to eat dinner; any meal time would suffice."

"I may be working on Saturday as well, I'm sorry. My weekends this month are pretty booked."

"What has you so busy that you can't squeeze in a meal with a friend?"

"Walker, I just met you. I hardly consider you a friend."

"Let me change that, Reese. By the time we are finished with our date, I will be so much more to you than a friend."

I grinned at him and smiled coyly. "You seem pretty sure of yourself, Walker."

"Oh I am, Reese, believe me. When I want something, I usually get it. I will work around your work schedule and anything else you have on your calendar." *Good lord! How could I resist his charm?*

"Okay. Friday night I have a job in Central Park. You can pick me up at seven. We can go to dinner after I wrap for the night."

"I'm confused, Reese, what exactly do you do for a living?"

"I model. I'm shooting a layout for fashion week. My best friend is one of the many designers that will be participating in the event." I looked over to my handsome stranger. His eyes brightened and his smile widened.

I couldn't help but feel excitement rage through my body as he lifted my hand to his mouth and kissed it. "Until Friday, Reese Mitchell."

Stunned into silence, I reached for my phone to call the other guy in my life. As expected, Freddy flipped out with my news. He was beyond happy that I had a date, especially with the handsome stranger.

I had to admit that I was excited about seeing him again. *Walker Reed... mm, mm, mm... Something about him just made my mind drift off to naughty places, and all I wanted to do was kiss and taste him. ...Whoa, what did I just say?* I never had a reaction to a guy like that before. I couldn't believe what I was saying, let alone thinking.

Of course, my mouth got the better of me, and I did say it out loud for Freddy to hear it.

"Ooh, Peaches, don't get shy on me now," Freddy said, while we he was helping me backstage. Then he jokingly growled at me like a cat. "I knew buried deep down underneath all of your southern belle charm, there was a sexy vixen dying to get out."

"You know that I love you, right?" I hugged Freddy and finished up with hair and make-up. I had three more outfits to get fitted into, and then I was done for the night. The photographers were amazing and made me feel at ease. Freddy's very revealing dress was the last one for me to walk out in. The crowd was very responsive to his line, and this dress was his signature piece. He designed his first wedding dress, but not traditional at all. It looked like it belonged on a rocker chick rather than a small town girl like myself, but I think I rocked it in my own way. Freddy insisted that I be the one to show it off. He said my body was made for this dress, and for me to go shake what the good Lord blessed me with.

Oh, I did. Rock music was blaring in the background as I met my theoretical groom at the end of the runway. He was wearing Freddy's version of a tux. He took my hand and twirled me around. I looked out into the audience, and that's when Walker's eyes found mine. I felt my body slipping when all thoughts went to Walker. He just smiled and winked. I gathered my composure and finished my sexy catwalk backstage to Freddy. I did one more turn, and then the audience erupted with applause. Freddy came rushing out along with the other models and blew kisses to the crowd. This was his moment, and I was so proud of him.

I quickly changed, but Freddy had other ideas for my date outfit. He insisted I wear one of his designs. He picked everything out for me to wear, and I was beyond excited for my date with Walker. My ensemble included a very tight, black pencil skirt with a lacy camisole and a half leather jacket. My heels skyrocketed me even taller than my 5'10 frame, but it was too late now to change. I had to hand it to Freddy. He had style, and he was sure to be a success.

As I exited the dressing tents, Walker was waiting for me. He looked amazing, dressed all in black. He looked downright edible. *Down girl, first things first.*

"Hey, Reese, you look fantastic." I could feel Walker's eyes traveling up and down my body with carnal hunger in his eyes. I wanted him, and my betraying body was telling him so.

"Hey, right back at ya. So what did you think of the show?" was all I could manage to say without revealing what I was really thinking.

"I didn't see all of it, but I did get the pleasure of watching you. I couldn't take my eyes off of you the entire time, but…you already knew that."

Before I could speak, Walker reached for me and pulled me forward against his rock hard chest. He crashed his mouth down on to mine, and swirled his tongue deep inside tasting me. I welcomed his kiss and returned the same level of intensity back to him. I heard a feral groan from his throat as he released my mouth. "I've wanted to do that since I first laid my eyes on you."

What was I going to say? Yes, and I've been waiting for you to do exactly that… and so much more. "Good, Walker, because I rather enjoyed that."

"Well, Ms. Mitchell. You will be enjoying much more from me before our evening concludes."

"Oh really, Mr. Reed."

"Yes, Ms. Mitchell, for many hours." That was my undoing. I almost wanted to run back to the dressing tent and change my now soaked panties. *How could this man arouse all these emotions in me?* Maybe Freddy was right. It was time to be brave and behave like a woman who wanted this man more than anything else.

Walker took me to an Italian restaurant in the Village. It was a small restaurant with only a few tables. I loved it because it wasn't loud or filled with many patrons. It had an intimate feel to it. We shared a bottle of wine, and I was surprised that I wasn't carded. I wasn't twenty one yet. The waiter filled our glasses, but not before

Walker sampled it first, and then gave him the okay to continue. I watched his mannerisms throughout the exchange. He was in total control, and just exuded confidence.

"So, Reese Mitchell, who are you? Tell me everything."

"Wow, you are direct."

"Yes, I am. I want to know everything about you. Obviously you are not a New Yorker from your accent. So let's begin there, shall we?"

"Okay Walker, I will give you the short version…for now. I'm from the Peach State, and before you ask, it's Georgia."

He smirked. "I knew that smart-ass, but continue please."

"I actually lived and grew up in a small town called Pottersville. It modernized over time, but it still holds the hometown feeling that I always loved. I lived with my grandparents, who still live there and own their own business. I attended my first three years of college at GSU, and then transferred here to New York for my senior year."

He looked uncomfortable in his seat, and I knew why. This was always the hard part of introductions. Why was I living with my grandparents? I ripped off the Band-Aid and explained to Walker before he had a chance to ask me. "My parents are deceased, and I lived with my grandparents since I was ten years old." *Okay, bring on the sad face now.* I waited for it, but all Walker did was take my hands in his and placed a gentle kiss on them. I went on to talk about Freddy and how we met and became best friends. I think Walker was relieved to discover that my best friend was gay, and not competition for him. I explained to Walker how close I was with Freddy, and whoever came into my life would have to accept our friendship. Walker, still holding my hands, let out the breath he was holding, and winked at me. "I don't like to share, Reese, but for you, I will try." He had nothing to be jealous about, but at the same time, it thrilled me. I had left out the bad parts that led me here to New York. I guessed that if this went anywhere with him, then I would eventually share my story.

"So Walker, now it's your turn. Tell me about your family." He was hesitant at first, but then began to speak.

"Reese, my family is nothing like yours. Clearly your family means a great deal to you. It's easily heard just by the way you speak of them. I can almost feel it in the way you describe every detail of your memories. I don't have that, and I never did. My parents are the complete opposite of yours. My mother, Olivia, is a pure bred. One hundred percent high society and lives up to every part of it. She's beautiful and graceful but blind to the world.

She only cares about her social groups, charities, and of course, the parties that we host in the Hamptons every summer. My father, Phillip, is master of the universe, and tries constantly to control my life. We own Reed Global. We build buildings. My father owns properties throughout New York City. I am to finish with my degree here, and then take my rightful place on the Reed throne."

"You don't want that, do you?"

"Yes and no. I want to take over for my father one day, but on my terms. By the time I graduate next May, I will have my business degree that my father has paid for, but what I really want to do is ar-chitecture. I have secretly taken classes that he doesn't know about, because I love it. I dream of seeing one of my designs come to life one day in a big city. Sure, we have the talent on our payroll, but I want to be included in that. He doesn't get it, never did, but when it's my turn to lead… he will."

After what we called our short versions of our introductions, we enjoyed our dinner and the comfort of each other's company. Once in a while, Walker would nudge me under the table, breaking me out of my gazing at him. He would wink at me and then smile. He was so beautiful, and my instincts were right on from the moment our eyes had met. We took a horse and carriage ride to conclude our evening. It was beginning to get chilly. Walker, feeling my shivers, wrapped his arms around me. We snuggled under the blanket that the driver provided, and we leaned in to each other. I breathed in his Armani cologne he was wearing. I remember this scent on some of the male models at the show. It smelled better on Walker.

With his hand holding mine, Walker escorted me to my door. Holding me in his arms, he gave me a kiss that would end all others. This time it was gentle and soft. His hands were cradling my face, and as our foreheads touched he whispered to me, "Thank you, Reese" and turned away from me to his waiting car. I blinked, and he was gone. *Where did he… what just happened here?* Needless to say, I was left with dejected feelings and the only thing to do next was to analyze it over a bowl of ice cream with Freddy.

I called out to Freddy, but our apartment was quiet. He had left a note telling me not to wait up or even expect him home tonight. Well, good for him, but now I'm left with all of my unanswered questions on how my amazing evening with Walker… abruptly ended in the strangest way. As I crawled into bed, my phone started buzzing. My eyes grew wide as I saw I had a text from Walker.

Walker: Your scent and taste are still on me, Reese. Don't over think anything tonight. I will see you tomorrow ;)

See me tomorrow? Is he nuts or something? How can he tell me to not over think it? He was the one that left, and with no explanation as to why the sudden escape act. I have to admit that I was curious to what would happen tomorrow, but not wanting to give him the satisfaction, I texted back.

Me: Sorry, I have other plans.

I hit the send button and immediately shut my phone off. *Screw that!* Yeah, I was playing games. I took a big step tonight with Walker, telling him about my family and lots of personal things. I never put myself out there for anyone. A couple of hours later, I still could not sleep. Curiosity got the better of me, and I turned my phone back on. Sure enough, a text was waiting for me from him.

Walker: Liar! ;) Who knew southern girls could be such vixens. I'll see you tomorrow…

Oh my god! Walker actually used the word "vixen." *Why did this excite me so much?* I guess I would find out tomorrow when I see him again.

By the time I managed to fall asleep it was dawn. It was way too early to be up, but no use going back to sleep now. I peeked into Freddy's room and the bed hadn't been slept in. I took a shower while the coffee brewed. By the time I walked back into the kitchen, there was Walker sitting at my table and drinking coffee with Freddy, who was wearing the same clothes from the night before, just a little wrinkled.

"Good morning, Peaches." Freddy blew me a kiss as he stuffed donuts in his mouth. Walker looked as amazing as he did last night, maybe even better. He was dressed casually in jeans and a Van Halen t-shirt.

Walking over to me, he took me in his arms and kissed me... He whispered in my ear, "A little taste for my vixen." With a swat to my ass, he turned and sat back down with Freddy. *What? What realm of crazy have I just walked in on?* I sat quietly while Freddy and Walker got to know each other. Freddy got up and rounded the table to me. "If anyone needs me, I will be sleeping for the next ten hours or so." That left me alone with Walker, and I wasn't sure what to think, seeing him sit here in my apartment. I was slightly upset with him... but I couldn't stop staring at his mouth and body.

"Don't over think it, Reese. You will just give yourself a headache. What happened last night? Is that what you want to ask me?" I sat silent, but nodded yes to him. "Why I left after I kissed you? If I had stayed... I probably would have taken you against the door frame." *What is it with this guy? I feel as if I am losing all logical thinking when I'm around him.*

"I'll have you know that I wouldn't have let our kiss goodnight go that far, let alone outside and up against my front door. You can stow that away in your fantasy file."

"You will, Reese. I have no doubt that you and I will be doing many things, on many surfaces."

"Wow, you are so full of yourself. And why do you think that I'm going to just roll over and turn into this sex crazed vixen for you? I hardly know you, Walker, and I don't know if I'd want you to be my fir…Shit!" *I so didn't want him to know that.*

"Wait a minute, hold up. You're a virgin? How? And why?" Now I'm pissed off. I couldn't believe I had to explain my virgin status to Walker, of all people. He is complete sex on a stick and I'm sure can get any woman he wants, but yet he sat there in my kitchen waiting on my explanation as to why I'm still a virgin. One answer came to mind. It's because of asshole questions like the ones Walker had just asked me.

"I think that's my business, Walker, and I don't care to tell you."

"You're wrong there, babe. It's my business now, because *you* are my business, and I want to know every last detail about you."

Before I could speak another word, Walker had me pinned up against the kitchen counter, and we were wildly kissing until we lost our breath. "I want you, Reese Mitchell, with every fiber in my soul. Looking at you makes my dick so hard, I just want to tear your clothes off right here and now. I'm lost in your gorgeous eyes and your mouth… my God! I never want to stop tasting you." Releasing my arms, he wrapped me up in his, leaving a trail of kisses down my neck. "I'm sorry if I was rough with you, that's not how I want to be with you, well at least not yet." I eyed him suspiciously, and of course he winked at me.

I decided to be bold and just say how I felt. It was obvious that Walker had no issues with telling me what he desired, so neither did I. "Walker, I want you too, but I'm not ready to sleep with you. My body may want to, but my mind and heart need to catch up a bit. I don't know how to describe how I'm feeling; is this what an instant connection feels like? Because if it is, I have never felt this way before, and I need to get a better handle on it."

"We can take it slow baby. As long as I know that you want me too, then we have all the time in the world."

We never made it out of my apartment. Walker and I spent all day locked in my room and shut the rest of the world out. We ordered in food and watched movies all day, along with talking and learning about each other. Lying in his arms with him wrapped around me felt amazing and safe.

I kept hearing Nana's voice in my head to not be afraid and live my life to the fullest. I was beginning to think that she had been right all along, and why was I waiting? I was twenty years old, and I'd never even been properly kissed until Walker. Yup…what the hell was I waiting for?

CHAPTER FOUR

Introductions...

THE ENTIRE DRIVE up to the Hamptons to meet Walker's parents had me tied up in knots. His father had been calling him non-stop for weeks now and asking what was taking up his time these days. Walker just blew him off and ignored him. That is until his mother phoned him and personally invited him to brunch. He had finally told his mother about me. She was curious to meet the woman in her son's life and extended the invitation to me as well.

I wasn't in any hurry to meet them. After Walker had told me about his father and how ruthless he can be, that left me feeling extremely uneasy. I wish we were making a trip to my hometown; he would love my grandparents, and they would welcome him with open arms. Nana was very excited for me when I called home to tell her my news. She said she didn't want to gloat, but she was right when she predicted that I would find my future husband here in New York. I told her to slow down and not plan the wedding yet. This relationship was new, and we were taking it slow. *And I mean slow*…Every time Walker touched me, I wanted to just peel his clothes off and make love to him. He kept telling me that we will have our time, and it will be even more amazing because we waited.

We entered through the tall, metal gates to the Reed property, and I could feel him beginning to get tense. Looking over at him with a reassuring smile, I squeezed his hand. He smiled back at me with apprehensive eyes, and pulled over to the side of the road.

"Reese, before you go in there, I have to warn you. It may feel like you are walking into the lion's den. My mother will welcome you, because she never faults on her manners, but my father will be an entirely different story. He is a snob, and not so nice. He is very direct, and does not care about how he speaks or the brash tone he will take with you. Ruthless… is an understatement where he is concerned. However, he's my father. I'm one of the few that can go up against him and still remain standing."

My stomach began to hurt after hearing Walker's testimonial speech about Phillip Reed. I never knew a person like this, but I was about to find out. Taking his hands in mine and kissing him sweetly on his very edible mouth, I said…"I will be fine. I'm stronger than you think, and I promise he won't scare me off."

"You say that now Reese, but you don't him like I do."

"Walker, then why am I here? Are you afraid he's going to tell me something that you don't want me to know?"

"Truth?" I nodded at him. "I love you Reese, so much that I'm afraid to blink and you're going to disappear." *What? Did he just say that he loves me?* "You are my air, I need you to breathe. You are my first thought when I wake in the morning, and my last thought when I go to sleep. When I hold you in my arms, my world feels right. For the first time in my life, I'm home."

He's looking at me for a response. My words are ready to burst from my mouth, but tears come first. Taking my seatbelt off, I lunged at Walker. I wrapped my arms around his neck, and began kissing him passionately to show him that I loved him too, so much.

"Babe, do you love me?" I began shaking my head as if I were having an anxiety attack. "I'm so happy right now. Reese, I need to hear the words from you. Do you love me?"

"Yes, Walker, with all my heart and soul, I love you… I love you and thank you for loving me." With his strong hands sliding through my hair, he kissed me hard, and I melted into him. It was as if we were one person. I would do anything for this man, and after his declaration of love, he was the keeper of my heart. Forever.

A tap on the window interrupted our moment. *Oh my god, please let this man not be his father.* Walker turned and told me that the man is security. I relaxed, and Walker rolled down the window to speak to the man. We are told that his father knows we are on the property and requests for us to drive up to the main house. Walker nodded, and we began driving again up the road that led to the private estate.

I quickly fixed my face and checked Walker's. He gripped my hand, and I pulled back to loosen it. "Relax baby, it's going to be fine." He winked, and we made our way to meet the parents. *Ready or not, here we come.*

"Well, it's about time, we thought you got lost." A beautiful girl welcomed us in, and Walker looked confused as to why she was there. "Elizabeth, what are you doing here?"

"I was invited. It's nice to see you too, Walker."

"I'm sorry. Forgive me, but I thought it was just going to be brunch with my parents."

"Well, my parents are also here. Our fathers played golf this morning, and I helped your mom with her planning for the cancer benefit luncheon she's hosting next week."

"I'm sure she appreciated that. Elizabeth, I would like to introduce you to my girlfriend, Reese Mitchell. Reese, this is my very good friend, Elizabeth Townsend."

Elizabeth was eying me up and down. I wasn't too sure what she was looking for, but I was raised with impeccable manners, so I extended my hand quickly to her. She shook my hand back, but with a bit of a tug. Walker never let my other hand break away from his, and we walked into the main room together.

"So far so good," I whispered to Walker as we made our way to the gardens where brunch had been arranged for us. The weather was gorgeous and not a cloud in the sky.

"Don't worry about Elizabeth; she's not the one you need to impress... Here we go."

"There's my handsome son, we've been waiting for you." His mother was beautiful, with her hair perfectly arranged in a pulled back chignon. I'd modeled enough designer clothes to know that she was wearing a $5000 Coco Chanel pant suit. Walker released me and pulled his mother into a tender hug. She welcomed him back, and placed a kiss on his cheek. She turned to me and smiled.

"Hello, my dear, I'm Olivia Walker Reed, and welcome to our home." Manners at their finest, I extended my hand to her, but she pulled me close and gave me two air kisses instead.

"Thank you for the invitation, Mrs. Reed. I'm Reese Mitchell."

"Call me Olivia. Come, let me show you the gardens. The colors are changing, and they are quite beautiful this time of the year." I winked at Walker and joined his mother for the tour. Elizabeth and her mother trailed behind us, as we continued to walk through the maze of flowers and designed shrubs and bushes. Olivia took my arm and folded it into the crook of her own.

"Reese, I want you to know that Walker speaks very highly of you, and I do believe he may love you. I love my son very much and will do anything to secure his future and his happiness. However, I must warn you to be careful." I stopped, and looked back at her with confusion. "Don't be alarmed dear; my words were not meant to scare you. They are meant as a warning. The Reed men can be very complicated and stubborn to the nines. They can be ruthless, but at the same time very loving." *There's that word again, ruthless.* "I'm sure you already have the impression that I'm just another member of the high society club and have no opinions when it comes to the world my husband lives in."

"Mrs. Reed...I don't think that-"

Holding her two hands up at me, she continued, "Let me finish dear. I know more than I'm credited for, and I want you to know that Walker has my blessing when it comes to the woman he loves. But having said that, my husband—as much as I love him—can

29

be…difficult. His father has certain expectations for Walker, and from the day I delivered him into this world, he had a destiny planned for him. You, my dear, may not be in that plan. So if you love my son back, like I believe you do, then stay strong. Let's join the men now for brunch, shall we?"

I simply answered, "Yes," and we made our way back. I needed a moment to digest all of what Walker's mother had just said to me. I asked where the bathroom was, and I was directed down a long hallway and down to a door on the left. I locked the door behind me, and I took some calming breaths. *What did Walker tell his mother about me? How does she know that I love him? I never said the words to her, and we didn't even have a real conversation. I just listened as she talked.*

And what's up with Elizabeth? That girl looks at Walker like I look at him. I'm not blind, she obviously has feelings for him, and maybe that's what I'm being warned about? Maybe I have some competition on my hands?

No use fighting my inner monologue at that moment, I had to re-join the party and make sure Elizabeth knew who Walker belonged to. As I walked back down the hallway, I'm surrounded by fine art and beautiful antiques. I stopped to look at a painting that caught my eye. *No way! It can't be.* I looked closer to examine the painting. It's an original painting of Picasso's earlier work. I was always intrigued by his Portrait of Dora Maar. She was his mistress during the war years in the twenties and thirties. I studied it closer and how and what she was portrayed in. Picasso painted her in a box that looked like she was confined. *Is this painting speaking to me like how Olivia did? Something about it makes me shiver with an unknown fear.* I broke my eyes away from the painting that seemed to be following me, but I stopped again when I heard raised voices coming from behind a closed door.

"You love defying me, Walker, don't you? Why is this insignificant girl here with you today? You had to know that Elizabeth would be here and with her family. Does it give you that much pleasure to embarrass me?"

"Yes, Father, I stay up night after night coming up with ways to humiliate you. Give me a small break. Mother told you that I was involved with someone, and she is not insignificant to me! I care for her very deeply, and I don't want to have this conversation again about who you think I should marry."

"We will have this conversation again and again until you understand your responsibilities. Elizabeth is your match in every way that matters. She is your thriving strength, standing and supporting you by your side."

"Yes, Father, she probably is, but she is not the one that I want. Elizabeth is my friend, has been my friend since we were kids; let's leave it that way." Walker turned to exit the room.

"Walker, this conversation is not over!"

"Yes, it is! It is for me. Now, if you will excuse me, my girl-friend is waiting for me. Oh, and Father? Be nice when you finally decide to grace us with your presence, I've spoken so 'highly' of you."

I quickly sprinted to the main room, and I'm escorted by house staff to re-join the other guests for brunch. I tried to get my trembling body under control, but it was futile at that point. Walker was so right about his father; how can he treat his only son in this manner? Walker did hold his own as he told me he could, but I still wanted to hold him. So I could tell him that I loved him for sticking up for me.

"Come on baby, we're leaving." Walker began to pull me out of my chair, when his father made his grand entrance. Not knowing what to do, I gestured at Walker to introduce me. He looked at me with fear in his eyes, but did what I asked. "I love you, Reese, please remember that."

"Well, this must be the lovely Reese Mitchell that I have heard so much about." His tone was mocking and sarcastic. He took my hand from Walker's and lifted it to his mouth to kiss it. "I'm Phillip Reed, welcome." That's all I got from him. I introduced myself after pulling my hand back, and we sat through a quiet brunch with minimal conversation.

Today had to be the most exhausting afternoon of my life. Walker was conveniently called away by Elizabeth and his mother, while I was left alone to talk with his father. *I love you Reese, please remember that.* Walker's words played through my mind as his father asked me for a moment of my time. I was trapped with no way of escaping this conversation. I had no choice but to hear him out.

"What are you doing with my son?" he asked.

"I would think that would be obvious, sir."

"Don't be smart with me, young lady, and answer my question."

"I wasn't trying to be rude sir, but I was raised knowing that if you ask a stupid question, then you deserve a stupid answer." *Bam! Score one for me.*

"Touché, dear, but no question is ever stupid, especially when it comes to my only son. I'm sure on your own level you are sweet, but from what I see is that you are not right for my son, and I would like you to stop seeing him." *He didn't just say that to me. What the hell? My level? Stop seeing Walker? Yeah, like that's going to happen.*

Counting to ten, and calmly reigning in my temper, I turned away from him to compose what I'm about to say to him. "Mr. Reed, you don't even know me, and for you to make demands of me is not only ridiculous, it's downright rude. You don't get to tell me anything, because you are nothing to me and I don't answer to you."

"Bravo, a woman with a backbone. For a minute there, I almost believed you, but I don't. You are a scared little girl, probably of your own shadow. You are clearly out of your league being here today with my son. Yes, I will give him credit for being brave enough to bring you here, but the only thing he has done is to further anger me. You don't want to tangle with me little girl. You had your fun with my son, now please do what I ask, and end it… now!" Before I could say another word, Walker came rushing back to my side and demanded we leave that minute. I didn't hesitate and never looked back at his father.

"I'm so sorry baby that you had to endure that. What did my father say? You must tell me everything." The speedometer was reaching ninety and climbing higher.

"Walker, please slow down before you get us killed. He didn't say anything that you didn't prepare me for. I held my own and didn't let him intimidate me." I wasn't going to say anything else about it to him tonight, maybe ever. My goal was to calm Walker down and put this entire disaster of a day behind us. We pulled up in front of my apartment and Walker walked around to open my door. I stepped out and into his arms. This hug felt different. I could feel his fear and desperation. I squeezed him as tightly as I could to reassure him that I wasn't scared off today.

"I love you, Reese. You have my heart, and I have yours."

"I love you too, Walker. Please don't worry about me. I'm fine, and this is the only place I want to be. Here and in your arms." He let out a sigh of relief and continued to hold me until Freddy interrupted us.

"Get a room!" he shouted. We both turned to look at him and we smiled. It didn't take a genius to figure out what was going through both our minds.

"I'll pick you up in two hours. Be ready, my love." He kissed me soundly and sped away.

Freddy came over to me and asked, "What's in two hours?"

I answered back, "The next step."

CHAPTER FIVE

Promises...

WITH THE SOUND of my doorbell, my stomach began doing flips. Freddy answered it to find Walker at my door with a dozen long stemmed red roses for me. I peeked out from my bedroom door, and then closed it quickly. I needed just a minute to calm my nerves before walking out. *I love this man, and I plan on showing him how much the minute we get out of here.*

Women usually don't call their grandmothers before making life changing decisions like the one I was about to do, but it's Nana, and I needed her. I'd been telling her everything about Walker. Well, almost everything, and she was beyond happy for me. Granddaddy of course wanted to size him up before giving me any blessings, but Nana made him clam up.

I left out the bad parts about how his father is trying to run me out of his life. Nana would go ballistic. She was very protective of me, and I had no doubt she wouldn't hesitate telling off Phillip Reed. No use on getting her blood pressure up, he was not worth anyone's time. Walker and I agreed to just ignore him and his rants.

"Knock, knock... You better be dressed by now, because you have a pacing boyfriend waiting on you."

"You can come in, Freddy. Just giving myself a quick look-over before I make my entrance."

"Woo-hoo! Reese, you look beautiful. Your man is not going to know what hit him."

"Thank you, Freddy, Let's hope I have a night to remember."

"Wearing that dress? You are off to a great start." I hugged my best friend, grabbed my clutch, and I went to Walker. He had his back to me when I entered the living room. He turned before I said anything, and I heard him take in a deep breath with the sight of me. My heart was already beginning to race as his eyes travelled all over my body. In two strides he had me swept up into his arms and was kissing me passionately. No words spoken, he was showing me how much he loved and wanted me. I quietly loved him back.

"Reese, you take my breath away. You look amazing, and I love this dress. I can't wait to peel it off of you, maybe with my teeth."

Walker had taken me to a French Restaurant, a first for me. I was apprehensive while looking at the menu, but Walker ordered for the two of us. He spoke fluent French to our waiter. Listening to him speak in a foreign language made me melt right in front of him. I could feel a throbbing between my legs, and I was completely turned on. I could have skipped dinner and gone right to dessert. Sliding his hand over my thighs, my body tingled under his touch. He remained quiet and studied my every move throughout dinner. Feeding me course after course, sometimes asking me to close my eyes. Walker's sexual ministrations were heating me up in all the right places, and I opened my eyes to see him completely focused on me. Taking my face in his hands, he kissed me, and snapped his fingers at the waiter. "Check please!"

Hurrying into Walker's building and completely ignoring his doorman's pleasantries, Walker kept a tight hold on my hand as he pulled me into the private elevator. Pushing me up against the cool walls, he began assaulting my neck with his amazing kisses. "I want you so badly, I can't wait to be inside of you."

My legs wobbled feebly underneath me and anticipation was flowing through my body. I wanted Walker as much as he wanted me. The doors opened and Walker swept me up into his arms, carrying me through his beautiful home. I wrapped my arms around his neck, and as he held me close to him, we felt each other's heartbeats. "I love you Reese, and tonight I'm going to make you completely mine."

He slowly let me down as he laced my neck with his soft kisses. I felt as if I just walked off one of those amusement rides where your body loses connection with gravity for a few seconds. I excused myself for a minute to freshen up. My eyes were bright, my cheeks were flushed with crimson, and my heart was beating rapidly. *This was it. Tonight I lose my long overdue virgin status. I am going to make love to the man I truly love. How many women get this chance to have what I have at this moment?* Feeling on top of the world, I didn't want to lose another minute away from him.

He had lit a fire in the fireplace in his living room. Soft instrumental music was playing in the background. He held his hand out for me. "Dance with me?"

Entwining our hands, he held me close. We swayed back and forth, never missing a beat between us. He slowly kissed me behind my ear and trailed his tongue down my neck, stopping at the base to place a love bite on my skin. "I want to mark every inch of you tonight, Reese. Your body is mine to do what I want with. I love every inch of it, and I want to see and touch every spot that makes you scream my name."

Oh holy hell! He was making me come undone right before him. My panties were soaked. This is the spell that he had cast over me. I was completely lost in him. I had no control over my senses and would easily submit to him. I so wanted to please him, but I had no clue how to. Self-doubt was slowly creeping up into my thoughts no matter how confident I tried to appear...

Reading me like a book, he took my hand and led me into his bedroom. "Don't worry baby we have all night, and we can take our time with each other." Tears pooled in my eyes, as I took in the room for the first time. He had candles lit, red rose petals strewn all around the room and on the bed. I noticed champagne chilling on a table accompanied with a platter of strawberries. There was a variety of chocolates on a beautiful silver platter by the bed. Walker had made sure that my first time was special.

My nerves were beginning to return. *I have no experience in this area; I give the word virgin a whole new meaning. I have never been with a man before, let alone on this intimate level. I tried when I was in college, but no one ever was worth giving that gift to. I guess I had pretty high standards, but those guys can't even come close to Walker. Here is this beautiful man standing before me, and all I can wonder is how did this happen? He is gorgeous, rich, can get any woman he wants, and he's here with a virgin from Georgia.*

"Stop over thinking again," he said, as if he was completely in tune with my inner deepest thoughts. He took me in his arms and calmed me with just his touch. "Reese, we don't have to do anything you don't think you are ready for. Just having you here with me is enough. I won't lie and tell you that I don't want you, because I do. I want you more than my next breath. You are completely breaking down my control."

Hanging my head low, I whispered, "I don't want to disappoint you."

He lifted my chin with his finger and looked deep into my glazed-over eyes. "Baby, that's impossible. I want you so much, and you are all that I see. Let me show you how much I adore and want the woman that has captured my heart. I have something for you."

"Walker, you don't have to give me any presents. You've done so much already." *He has that look in his eyes, again. What is he up to?*

"Indulge me please? This present may be more for me than for you, my love. Close your eyes." I quietly obeyed and did what he asked of me. I heard him move about the room until he sat beside me, and he instructed me to open my eyes. He had placed a silver wrapped box on my lap with a black ribbon tied around it. Of course I wanted to tear it open before him, but I waited for him to give me permission to do so.

"Do you want your gift now?"

"Yes"

"Then please... open it." I carefully untie the elegant wrapped bow and lifted the many layers of tissue paper that concealed what I now know must be lingerie. My eyes glanced down to the most beautiful corset I had ever seen. I glided my hand over the material; it felt luxurious and expensive. It was the most striking color of emerald green that I had ever seen. It was made of pure silk and French lace. He had also bought me stockings and a garter.

"Walker, it's...stunning."

"I hope it's not too much, but when I saw you model in something similar to this, I had to see it again, but only in my private company. Reese, you are exquisite, and your body should only be covered in the finest material. I want you to wear this for me, and I want to take my time peeling it slowly off your body."

"I'll be just a minute." I carried the box and went back into his bathroom. Half my apartment would fit into here. I steadied my rapid breaths, and I changed out of my dress and into this beautiful lingerie he had chosen for me. He certainly knew the art of seduction. I silently prayed that he didn't do this for all the women he had been with. *Silly girl, stop it. I trust Walker completely, and I have never wanted anything more than this moment with him. No more doubtful thinking.* My doubts had been banished with all of his declarations he made to me tonight. I took one last look at myself in his full length mirror. The corset fit me like it was made for me and me alone. I shook out my hair, and it looked wild as it cascaded down my shoulders. *He's going to lose his mind when he sees me, but maybe that was his intention all along.* I opened the door and made my way back to him. He was standing before me, sans his shirt and socks. He was magnificently naked from the waist up; even his feet were downright sexy bare.

Walker was eyeing me while I stood before him. I went to touch him, but he stopped me. "Step back, let me look at you." I did, and then he instructed me to turn for him. I felt free and unashamed. He looked like a hungry tiger ready to pounce on his prey. "You are so beautiful, Reese. Come here." He tilted his head as he crooked his finger, motioning for me to come to him.

I wrapped my arms around his neck and pulled him down onto my lips. I swirled my tongue deep within his mouth, and he sucked on mine. He let out feral groans as we tasted each other. Walker fell to his knees and stroked his hands up and down my thighs. "I love how silk feels on your legs, baby. I think we will leave these on with your four inch 'fuck me' heels."

He gripped my ass and inhaled my scent through my panties, biting the delicate lace that he then shred with one forceful tug. "I can't wait to be inside of you, but first I need a taste." I think I came right there. He winked at me, swiftly lifted me up, and carried me to his massive bed. I'm placed in the middle, and he stripped himself of his clothing, while never taking his eyes off of me.

"You are so beautiful, Walker. Every inch of you is perfect."

"Oh baby, you haven't even seen the best part yet," and with that, his enormous throbbing penis was released. He smiled at my reaction and again read my thoughts. "Don't worry baby, you'll be able to take all of me in your beautiful pink pussy."

Oh I hope so, because that thing looks like it has the power to split me in two. I quickly sat up to touch him, and he gripped my hands. "One step at a time… just let me love you."

His skillful fingers were still perusing my body, and I waited with anticipation on what he would do next. He took my protruding nipple into his mouth and began to suck on it between his teeth. The noises that escaped me I had never heard before. I screamed out in pleasure, but he silenced me with his tongue. He gave my other breast the same treatment. He sat back on his knees and gently pushed my legs apart. He dipped his head low to lap at me with his skillful tongue. I bucked my hips up at him, and he continued to work me over with his mouth. In moments, my hands instinctually reached for his head to pull him down deeper into me. I arched my back, gripped the sheets, and began to experience the most earth shattering feeling I had ever felt in all my life. "Let me hear you, Reese. Scream my name. Who do you belong to?"

"Walker! I belong to you... only you!"

"Damn straight, you do. Come for me baby. I want to taste your sweetness. I want to feel your quivers on my hand and know that it's me doing that to you. Come Reese...come," he whispered. Oh I did, the spasms pulsed through my body as if I just touched a live wire. He was lapping my juices up until he was satisfied. I orgasmed again and again. Walker's mouth was now on mine. I tasted myself on him. It was beyond erotic and sinfully delicious. In an instant I had transformed into the vixen Walker made me feel like. I didn't care about the naughtiness behind the word anymore, I wanted to be everything and anything for Walker.

He ran his hands up and down the lacy material that covered my body, slowly undoing each button until it was completely open. I was as still as a statue as he slipped it off and tossed it to the floor. He again ran his hands up my thighs feeling the soft silk, as he reached the top of my swollen clit, inhaling my scent and kissing all the spots he had just marked. He sat up and stared at me, memorizing every inch of my body. With only wearing my stockings and shoes, I laid there bare and exposed for him. No words spoken between us, Walker crawled up toward me and opened my legs apart with his. He gave a sexy wink, a hint of wickedness in his eyes and bent to enter me again with his tongue. I clutched the sheets for support as he lifted me higher and higher. Inserting one finger, and then two, he worked me over until the sensation was building within me again. *Oh my god, how much more can I take? This man knows no bounds, and I love it!*

Feeling this immeasurable amount of pleasure and excitement, I screamed his name again, even louder than before. I come again and again as he continued to work me over with his mind-blowing tongue. "Open your eyes, baby. Are you okay?" he asked. I simply nodded my answer with no ability to speak. I was so caught up in him and just wanted more. He kissed me all over my chest and neck until he reached my mouth. Having tasted m myself already once tonight on his lips, it ignited me once more. I wanted to pleasure him, but he held my hands and told me tonight is for me, and me alone. *I want him inside of me, now! I'm ready!* He cupped my face and kissed me once more. "You are mine, Reese Mitchell. I love you... Forever."

He took out a condom from his side table and began to open it. He showed me how to place it on him. I was in shock that everything felt so natural with him. It was like I'd done this with him before. As I guided the condom down, all I felt were the veins pulsating on his dick and the strength behind his long length.

I gasped a bit not knowing what to do next. Walker sensed my hesitation and told me that it would be okay, and I would stretch as he enters me. "Baby, although this is not my first time, it is my first with a virgin. Thank you so much for letting me be yours, and I promise to go slow." With his body hovering over mine he gently rubbed his penis in my folds. *He's getting me ready, and I appreciate the thoughtfulness but I NEED to have him inside me!*

I tried to relax as he slowly entered me. With the first contact, my body tightened around him. "Keep your eyes open, baby. I need to know if I'm hurting you." *He's not, it's just a little uncomfortable, but I'm getting used to it.* He slowly went deeper and deeper. I felt a pinch as he completely entered me, and I let out a shriek. My eyes were filled with tears, and he stopped completely.

But I didn't let him stop. I slowly moved my hips, grinded into him, and told him that I'm fine. With the reassurance that he needed to see, he went deeper and began to move faster. Wrapping my legs around his waist, my heels were digging into his very tight and round ass. "Oh god Reese...YES!" He grunted a bit with the heel pinching into his skin but didn't stop. Telling me over and over again how much he loved me, he gripped my hands and we both let go of our orgasms, coming together. I could feel our pulses beating in time with each other. Walker was the one now screaming, and it was music to my ears. Our skin was wet with sweat. He was panting on top of me. Eventually, I had to nudge him; he is so strong, but heavy. "Sorry babe, I needed a minute to catch my breath." I smiled, and he pulled out of me, making me wince a bit.

Wrapping our bodies around each other, he pulled the comforter over us, and I drifted off into a contented sleep thanking the heavens for my happiness, and for Walker. He held me for the entire night. *I'm so in love with this man.*

Dreaming of making love with Walker last night kept me rooted in place. I didn't want to wake up, but something hard nudged me from behind. I opened one eye at a time, and smiled and felt his warm breath on my neck. "Good morning, baby," he crooned in my ear. *His voice alone can make any woman lose all of her senses.* I rolled over to face my beautiful man smiling back at me.

"Good morning to you too! Sleep well?" I ask him.

Pulling me on top of him so we are nose to nose, he kissed me and rolled his delicious tongue over my lips. "I think you already know how well I slept, but if you need a reminder on how I got to my level of relaxation, then I can easily show you again."

"Um...yes, I think I need a reminder, because I can't seem to remember too much about it."

Now with a wicked gleam in his eyes, he flipped me over and began reminding me. With me on my stomach, Walker pressed his body into my back. He was fucking me into the mattress, and making sure I felt every inch of his hard length pushing inside me. I clenched around him and screamed his name in pure ecstasy. My orgasm continued to riddle my body with spasms as Walker collapsed on top of me.

"Are we on the same page now?" he asked. I giggled into my pillow, and he flipped me again as if I weighed nothing. He was so strong, and I loved how he did things so effortlessly.

"Oh yes, we are clearly on the same page."

We kissed and kissed until the rumbles of our stomachs broke our connection. "What time is it?"

He looked over and told me it's almost ten. I sat up in shock that I slept in that late. I had never slept past eight o'clock, and that was on a weekend.

"It's okay baby, we have all day, and we have nowhere to be. Relax and come lay back down with me."

"I will after I freshen up." I gave him a quick peck on his lips, and I hurried to his bathroom, dropping my sheet along the way so he could catch a glimpse of my ass he held many times last night. I heard him growl as I closed the door behind me. Looking at my reflection in the mirror, I noticed that my hair was totally sexed out with tangles and knots. My face was flushed, and my lips were swollen. I could feel the swells of my breasts as I took in my appearance.

Walker transformed me into a woman overnight. He was an amazing lover and although he wasn't as gentle with me this morning, he was very sweet and oh so careful with me last night. He took his time as he explored my body. He gave me pleasure that I had never experienced in all of my life. Yes, we shared many firsts, and I couldn't wait to see what was next.

CHAPTER SIX

Leap of faith...

AFTER SEVERAL MORE rounds of incredible and hot sex, my body was well sated. We were both entangled in each other while we were lying in front of the fireplace in the living room. He fed me strawberries and licked off drops of chocolate that he conveniently dripped down my breasts. I didn't want to come down from this high that I was on. Somehow he became so in tune with my body and all it said to him without ever using a word.

"Stop over thinking again, Reese," he said. *How does he do this? And how does he know that I'm over thinking anything?* "Reese, I love you, and I plan on building my whole future around you... if you'll have me."

"What are you saying to me, Walker?"

"What do you think I'm saying, Reese?"

"Are you asking me to marry you?" He smiled and brought me closer to him in his arms.

"Well, not today, but yes, my love. When I look to my future and all it can be, the only person I want to share my life with is you. After we graduate in May, my next step is to move on to California. My father is grooming me to take over at Reed Global. He's wanted to expand out to the west coast for years now, and he wants me to take over as CEO."

"Walker, I haven't even thought about what is next for me. On top of going to graduate school, I have been offered to continue modeling for Elite, but that's not what I want as my career. I want to teach, and I still have several years of school before I get the position I truly want."

"Reese, you can have it all. I don't doubt that. I was just hoping that you would do those things in California with me. I know it's a huge step, a leap of faith, but it's our chance. I'm hoping you say yes."

"Walker, we have only been together for a few months, you haven't even met my family yet. I still have so much to tell you about my life and my home in Georgia. Now you just ask me to pick up what I have here in New York, and go with you to California? What about your father? I don't think he will be exactly pleased with you and your plans to marry the country bumpkin."

Walker's eyes go to a fiery halt now. "Did he call you that? When did he hurt you Reese? I swear to god, I will tell his ass off."

"Calm down. He didn't use those exact words, but he made it perfectly clear that he has a plan for you. One that doesn't include me, Walker. I think he would be happier if you were marrying…what's her name? Elizabeth."

"My father can plan all he wants for me, Reese, but he doesn't get that control over me. He never will. Please don't let him scare you off. Elizabeth is my friend, my friend since childhood. We fooled around when we were teenagers, and it felt like I was kissing my sister. We both agreed how silly we were and vowed to remain friends, nothing more. My heart belongs to you, Reese, it has since the first day I saw your beautiful face."

"Does she know that, Walker? Because if you ask me, she's clearly in love with you, babe, and she's waiting in the wings for you."

"She can wait all she wants; it doesn't mean she gets to have me. I love you and only you. Trust me when I say these words to you, that they have one hundred percent truth behind them. As far as knowing more about you, I know everything I need to know. I would love to meet your family. When is your birthday, Reese?"

I smiled with the knowledge that it was coming up very soon, and he waited for my answer. "I was born on December twenty third, two days before Christmas."

"That is so perfect, Reese. How about we travel to Georgia for your birthday and Christmas?" My heart was about to spill over with all that he had said to me. He never took his eyes off of me, as he once again declared his love.

"That would be amazing for you to join us for Christmas. I can't wait to call Nana and tell her the good news. How will your family feel about you missing the holidays with them?"

"My parents always travel around Christmas; I don't think they will care. They do plan a New Year's Extravaganza at their pent-house in the city. That event, my appearance will be required, but we can skip out early... We can have our own private celebration later." We kissed, made love for the rest of the day, and then Walker finally drove me home. He wanted me to stay with him, but I had no clean clothes with me. I also had an early morning class.

"There she is, my roommate doing the walk of shame, and at this hour." Freddy teased me, as he looked at his invisible watch on his wrist.

"If that's what you call it, then by all means I walk it proudly." I tried to sprint across the room to Freddy's waiting arms, but my muscles were sore from the vigorous workout Walker put me through. Freddy could read me like a book, and he was grinning with delight. Pulling me down to the sofa, he wanted details, and I was not to leave one part out or he won't let me sleep.

I promised to tell him everything, but he would have to wait until tomorrow afternoon. I needed to shower and get some sleep. He wasn't happy that he had to wait but gave me a kiss on my cheek as I walked away to my bedroom. I was out cold, and I nearly missed my alarm after it went off several times of me hitting the snooze button.

Freddy had to jump on my bed to get me up, almost knocking me onto the floor.

I made it to class on time, but just by a few minutes. I felt like I was on a sex hangover. My thoughts went straight to Walker, causing the aching throb between my legs to pulsate. *Oh I wanted to see him, and now! Show some restraint girl. You promised Freddy, your best friend, a catch up night with wine and pizza.*

I only had morning classes, and no work scheduled for today. My day was done. I was heading for home when I was stopped by a well-dressed man in a chauffeur's uniform. This guy looked like a character from an old time movie. He put his hands up to me, signaling me that he wasn't a threat; he just wanted to deliver a message to me.

"My name is Ralston, and I work for Mr. Reed. He has asked me to drive you to his office, where your presence is required." I froze where I was standing. Mr. Reed's driver had to be 6' 4 at least, and large in size. All my defenses were up and judging by how intimidating Mr. Reed can be, I wasn't taking any chances with his driver. He said he didn't mean any harm, didn't me to alarm me, and he was only doing his job. Job or not, he was scaring me. No way in hell was I going anywhere with him, and especially to see Walker's father.

With all the courage I could gather, I told him no. "Mr. Ralston, if Mr. Reed wants to speak with me, he can find me at his son's apartment where I will be for the rest of the day." I moved past him and walked as fast as I could to the subway. *He didn't follow me, thank you God.* I clearly was lying to him, but I think he believed me. I was sure that he would scurry back to Mr. Reed with my reply. I hurried home and called Freddy right away. He shortened his day and came right home. By the time Freddy arrived, I had dinner waiting, and I was well into my second glass of wine.

Freddy didn't hesitate to scoop me up into his arms, and he held me until I stopped shaking. I was so scared that everything I was building here in New York and with Walker was about to come crashing down on me. The boulder was Phillip Reed.

"Okay baby girl, let's take a breath, and tell me everything about this asshole. How did you end up on his bad side, and why is he gunning so hard to fuck with you?"

"One question at a time, friend. Okay, the bottom line is that he doesn't like me, he doesn't want me with his son, and I don't fit into whatever plan he has for Walker. Walker has told me time and time again that I am to ignore his father and his would-be threats, but I can't, Freddy. Not after he sent a driver for me. I already told Walker about my first meeting with him, and he flipped out. I can't come between him and his father. I would never forgive myself, Freddy. A relationship that a child has with their parents is precious, an unbreakable bond. I had that with my own, but now they're gone. I can't be responsible for coming between Walker and his father. I just won't do that to him, Freddy."

"Reese, from you have told me about the Reed family, they are just another rich and high society New York City family that likes to throw their money around and try to step on people that are not worthy of them. You are making them out to be this perfect idealistic family, a family who is close and shares in each other's lives. God forbid their son decides to choose outside of their circle and run the risk of their empire crumbling around them. Reese, please tell me you don't see them any other way?"

Whispering into Freddy's chest, I say, "Walker is different." I sensed my friend's doubt. I looked up in to his eyes, and tried to convince him otherwise. "He is, Freddy, and that is one of the reasons why this is so hard. If I tell him how his father has been behaving, then it will only cause him pain. It will hurt him. I will be forcing Walker to make a choice between his family and me. I won't do it, Freddy. No matter what kind of father Phillip Reed is. He's still his parent, and where I come from… that matters."

"You know you're right about one thing, Reese. A bond between children and their parents should be unbreakable and special, but not all families are like that. I love my mishpakhe very much, but

I would never let them tell me how to live my life. Especially now that I'm a grown man. Judging on how you're looking at me right now, I've confused you with another slang word. Sorry, Peaches. It means family."

"It's okay, Freddy. I knew that one. My mind is just all over the place right now."

"Reese, my parents mean the world to me, but having said that, I still can't allow them to control me. Why do you think I came out when I did? They wanted me to marry, take over one of their many businesses, have kids, and shine in the synagogue. I always knew who I was, and although I didn't fulfill their original hopes and dreams for me, I've done it in other ways. If you want my advice, you should be honest with Walker. Tell him the truth. He is a grown ass man, and he doesn't look like the type to just cave in to make "Daddy" happy. Don't be afraid, baby girl. If you want this man and truly want a future with him, then Woman Up. Tell him what the hell is going on."

I hugged my best friend tighter and felt so much better after our talk. "Thank you, Freddy. You always know the right advice to give me. I love you, and I will tell him the first chance I get."

"Tell me what?" Freddy and I both jumped off the couch in surprise, when we heard the front door slam shut. Walker was looking at the two of us, and his facial expression was glacial as he eyed our compromising position that we were in. I leapt out of Freddy's arms and right into his, showing him exactly who I belonged to. I never saw Walker jealous before, and he never had to be when it came to Freddy. Freddy was my best friend and nothing more.

"I didn't expect to see you tonight." My voice was cracking as I looked up into Walker's eyes. He was quiet, and still looking over to the couch. "Walker, talk to me, are you okay?"

"Yes, I'm fine. Why wouldn't I be okay? I come over to my girlfriend's home to see her wrapped around her…what do you call each other, Reese…best friends?" The tone in his voice was rude and sarcastic. I didn't like it one bit, and it was very Phillip-like at the moment.

Freddy, not wanting to have a confrontation with the man I love, simply put his hands up and walked into his room. He was hurt by Walker's suggestions, but I was left to deal with it. "Walker, you can't just come in here and overreact to something that is completely innocent. I had a rough day, and Freddy was just helping me work through it. Why are you behaving like this? Freddy is like a brother to me, and you have no reason to be jealous or accusatory."

"How do you *expect* me to react? When I see the woman that I love tangled up with another guy?"

"You can't be serious right now, Walker. Let's forget about his personal preference for the moment, and go back to one of our first conversations you and I had. I told you that Freddy is my best friend, and at the time, was my only friend here in the city. He is very important in my life and if you have a problem with that, then we shouldn't be together."

"Reese, why were you in his arms?" Walker asked quietly.

"I believe I already told you why. I was having a bad day, and Freddy was there for me."

"I'm your boyfriend, Reese. If you need a shoulder to cry on, then it should be mine. Secondly, if you don't want me just stopping by, then you shouldn't have given me a key." I broke away from him and his coldness to show him the door. He stood there looking at me, still holding flowers. "Are you asking me to leave?"

"NO, I'M TELLING YOU TO LEAVE! It's obvious you want to continue to behave like an adolescent and choose to unfairly judge my relationship with my best friend. If you're not going to behave like the man I know you are, then yes, here's the door. Don't let it hit you in the ass on your way out."

Dropping my flowers, he took two strides and then had me pinned up against the door. He was savagely kissing me and holding me in place. I returned the same level of passion he was giving me with his wet kisses. His hard length was pressing into me, and I began to cry out in pleasure.

"No one, and I mean no one, has ever spoken to me like that before," he grunted. "I fucking love it, and I want you so much that I'm about to take you right here."

"Bedroom," I said breathlessly. Picking me up and throwing me over his shoulders, that is exactly where we went but not before slapping me hard on my ass. He laid me out on my bed and stripped us both bare. Without a second thought, he had me wide open and he was between my legs, pleasuring me with his tongue until I could take no more. Screaming his name, I said, "Fuck me please... now Walker." He handed me a condom, and I practically tore it open with my teeth. I slid it down his hard length, then he slammed into me with such a strong force, I let out a whimper. Then it was pure wanton pleasure and a thrill ride he was taking me on. Higher and higher my body was climbing, until my orgasm rocked my body. I spasmed over and over again. *Oh shit! What about Freddy right in the next room? Too late to be embarrassed now, I just hope he is wearing his headphones.*

Now that my man had been sated with angry sex, he slept soundly holding me tight. I ever so gently wiggled my way out from underneath his heavy limbs to go find Freddy.

My friend must have been out of his mind with worry. Freddy gave me a look that screamed that he was worried but he trusted my judgment, and I knew I could trust Walker. Freddy was seated at the table and eating pizza. "Hungry?" he asked, "You must be with all that rigorous exercise you just did." *Yup...he heard us, how could he not on account of how loud we were.* "You have to tell him Reese, and you have to do it tonight. I'm sorry, but what his father is doing to you is not right, and your boyfriend needs to put a stop to it. For god's sake, he sent one of his goons out to get you!"

Before I could answer him, Freddy had one more thing to say. "I had my reasons why I wanted to spend some alone time with you tonight." My heart tightened as I watch my friend struggle with his words. Not being able to look me in the eyes he said, "I've been given the chance of a lifetime to work in Milan as a protégé to Ralph

Lauren."

"Wow! That is amazing, Freddy. When did you find out?"

"I've actually known for a couple of weeks now, but there was never a good time to tell you. Reese, this means that I will be moving to Milan, and that means leaving you." That hit me like a punch to my stomach. Freddy was my best friend, and my only true friend that I trusted everything with. We have shared so much with each other, and since we met back in Georgia, we have kind of been a team.

"Hey! Where did you go Peaches?" I looked up into Freddy's eyes, while mine filled with tears. I jumped right into his arms, and hugged him.

"I suck as a best friend, and I don't know how you put up with me. I should have been here for you when you wanted to share your good news. I'm sorry. I've been so wrapped up in my relationship with Walker that he is all I see these days, and you should be pissed about how I have blown you off."

"Well, Peaches… you blew something!"

"Freddy!" I shrieked in embarrassment. "I can't believe you just said that. How can I even look at you with a straight face?"

"Let's break it down, Peaches. One… don't ever be embarrassed, especially with me and about sex. Two… what did you expect me to say after your wall banging romp with your hot man? Three... I am far from straight, so please let me have my fun for a little while longer?"

"I love you, best friend."

"I love you more. Now let's talk about the angry hot man that is passed out in the next room. Reese, from what I see, he loves you. He clearly is protective of you, and the way he looked at me when he arrived here tonight speaks volumes on how he feels about you. That guy wanted to put some hurting on me, best friend or not. He's a guy that saw another guy's hands on his woman. He's in deep Peaches, and so are you. He is the first person other than me that you have let in, so don't shut him out now." Freddy knew me better than anyone, and I knew he was right.

"Okay Freddy, I will. You're always right, and I promise to talk to him. Do you mind giving me some time alone with him?"

"Not at all. I'm meeting up with some friends in the Village. I saved you some pizza. Call me if you need me." One more hug to Freddy, and I made my way back to Walker. I slowly opened my bedroom door and found Walker sitting up with his back to my headboard. The sheet was barely covering his beautiful muscled body.

I took in every inch of him, as wetness pooled between my legs, and my mouth thirsted to taste him. I took his face in my hands, kissed him, and showed him how much I loved him. I kissed my way down to his hard, throbbing dick. Going on natural instinct, I looked up at him while I let my tongue slide up and over his bulbous head. His scent was intoxicating. I let my hand wrap around him and guided his cock into my mouth while pumping it. I loved the taste of him, and I could feel him leaking pre-cum. My mouth dripping with saliva all the way to the base. I started to move slowly. Then it was if I couldn't get enough…I was ravenous for him.

He reached down and held my head, guiding me up and down his length. I could feel his balls tightening. He was getting close. When I thought he was going to come, he pulled me up and flipped me to my back. He whispered, "I need you so much baby, please let me love you."

"Yes, I need you too. Love me, and love me now."

The conversation that needed to happen would have to wait until morning. Walker took me all night long, until my sensitive bud throbbed so much after our aggressive love making, that I could do no more. Our sweaty bodies soaked through my sheets. He carried me into the shower and washed me from head to toe, not missing one ounce of me. I loved showers with him, but I was exhausted and he knew it. After making up my bed, we fell into each other.

I placed my head on his chest and listened to the drums of Walker's heartbeat. It was fast at first, and then with each beat, it slowed down. I knew he was sleeping. My mind was over stimulated, and I knew I shouldn't be afraid, but I was. We were so different and had completely different backgrounds. I still questioned how we were together, but from the beginning Walker had shown me that he didn't care about anyone's opinions. Freddy was right, I had to trust my heart in Walker's hands and let him in. Taking in some calming breaths, my eyes finally began to close; I drifted off into peaceful sleep with my beautiful man holding me.

He moved only once and kissed the top of my head. He knew me so well already. *How did this happen? How could I be so lucky?*

I heard him say, "Don't over think it babe. I love you."

I whispered back, "I love you too, Walker. So much."

CHAPTER SEVEN

The truth hurts...

ROLLING OVER TO find his side of the bed cold and no Walker in sight, I quickly got up to look for him. Pain was constricting around my heart for some strange reason. *Why am I thinking he's gone, and last night was his way of saying goodbye to me? Am I just this clueless girl that his father thinks I am?* Wrapping my arms around myself, there was no sign of Walker throughout my apartment. I looked again for maybe a note he might have left, but nothing. Until I heard my front door open and close.

There he stood, my beautiful man holding two bags of delicious smelling baked goods and coffee. I took the picture of him in, and all of a sudden the dam burst with my tears falling fast down my cheeks. I turned away from him, and ran to lock myself in my bathroom. He called out to me, but I ignored him. I cried until there were no more tears. Walker demanded that I open the door for him or he was going to kick it in. I splashed cold water on my face, opened the door, and just hung my head.

"Reese, what the hell? What is going on with you, and why are you crying? I'm so sorry for behaving the way I did last night. I thought we had resolved this and we are okay." Staring at my feet so that he had to lift my chin to look at me, he said, "Babe... please tell me what's wrong?"

I buried my face in to his chest. His intoxicating scent calmed me. I whispered the words that made my mouth taste like vinegar, "It's your father."

"What about my father? Has he done something to upset you? Please tell me Reese, and do not leave out any details."

Now that I had said the words to him, he waited for me to explain. I felt sick to my stomach that I had to have this conversation with him. We walked to the couch, he handed me my coffee and a scone. It smelled delicious, and I felt guilty for even thinking he was leaving me, while all along he was simply getting us breakfast. I couldn't resist the pastry, so I took a couple of bites before talking with Walker. He smiled at me knowing his kind gesture had made me happy. I put down my coffee to take hold of Walker's hands. "This is hard for me to say to you because I never want to be the one that hurts you, but you do need to know."

"Reese, you say you don't want to hurt me, then prove it. Please tell me that you love me, and only me. What did I walk in on yesterday? You say it's about my father. You must tell me how that bastard hurt you. I swear to god that he will never have the opportunity to do that again!"

"I love you… I want you… and only you! I'm afraid that we are up against something far too big for either one of us to handle. Your father has made it perfectly clear that I am not his choice for you, and he will stop at nothing to rid me from your life. He wants me to end things with you and hand you over to Elizabeth. He sent his driver for me yesterday. I was so scared that I ran from him and came straight home."

"Are you fucking kidding me? He sent Ralston?"

"Yes, I believe that was his name. He said he didn't mean to scare me, but he was to deliver me to your father at his office for a meeting."

"Oh hell no, that will never happen. Did he touch you, Reese?" I shook my head no at him. "Reese, I can't even begin to tell you how sorry I am that he is such an asshole, and he is still trying to run my life. Please, babe, you have to trust me and trust that I will take care of this. I will end this bullshit today!"

"Walker, how are you going to do that? He will cut you off, and then where will you be? You have to finish school and become all the great things that you are destined to be. I won't be the reason you jeopardize your future."

"That stubborn man who I share blood lines with has no idea about who the hell I am. He has only his way of thinking, and he only wants to control people. He never listens to anyone else! That is going to change, believe me."

"Walker, I can't compromise your life and what has been planned for you."

Cutting me off and holding my now wet face in his hands, he said, "Reese, I might as well let my father cut me down at my knees, because if I lose you, then my future is fucked anyway. Everything that I thought I wanted before meeting you has become an after-thought. When I look at you, this is what I see. I see you walking down the aisle in a beautiful, white dress designed by Freddy, and escorted by your grandfather. You'll look so beautiful that I can hardly breathe. I see you holding our newborn son or daughter in your arms. I kiss your lips, and whisper thank you for making me the happiest man in the world. I see you and our children by my side when I cut the ribbon to the new building that I have designed. I see us growing old together, Reese. We will enjoy the family that we created. We will welcome our grandchildren into the world. Forever, baby… I only see forever when I look at you. That's the future I want Reese, and I will not let my father take that away from me, or us. Please believe me, and tell me right here and now that you want it too."

He didn't have to ask me twice, of course I want this with him, how can I not? I love him so much, and although it has only been a short time for us, sometimes you just know when it's perfect. Walker is my perfect, and I believe every word that he has said to me. I will face his ruthless father with Walker holding my hand. I promise not to be intimidated by Phillip Reed again. We made passionate love, sealing our commitment to one another. Walker kissed me goodbye tenderly. I hated to see him leave, but I knew where he needed to go.

Freddy came home a few hours later, and I told him everything that happened with Walker. He was relieved that we worked things out and that Walker knew everything that was going on with his father. My stomach was doing flip flops, I was so nervous. I glanced over to the time on the clock. It had been hours since he left, and I had heard nothing from him. I was about to dial his number when I heard my front door open. Walker was coming through it as if he lived here for years. Not waiting for him to take his coat off, I rushed to his side. I wrapped my arms around his waist and held him.

He just sighed and held me close. We stood there for what seem like forever until he broke our connection and he guided me back to my bedroom. He dropped his wallet and keys, kicked off his shoes, and stripped down to his boxers. The sight of him made my heart just speed up with want for him, but I think he needed something else from me tonight. I slipped out of my clothing and took his hand. We wrapped ourselves around each other and said nothing. Walker just kissed me and held me in his arms throughout the night.

Whatever happened with his father, he clearly wasn't ready to share with me. I only acted on his signals and knew when he was ready… I would be here to listen. I was just praying that he didn't change his mind about us.

I looked over to my side table to check the time, and my clock blinked five a.m. Oh this godly hour, but we did go to sleep early, so my eyes were wide awake. Walker was still asleep, but something else was awake on him. I gently began stroking his hard length, and ever so carefully guided his boxers down, releasing his hard erection. I so wanted to pleasure him this way. He only let me a couple of times before, and always wanted to let me be on the receiving end. Not this morning. It was my turn to rock his world, and I wouldn't allow him to stop me. I took him deep into my mouth as I used my hand to stroke up and down his hard length, massaging him underneath his heavy balls. He moved his hips while he groaned out his cries of pleasure. He wasn't stopping me. He was encouraging me to continue and take in all of him. I did that and more until he exploded into my mouth. I let the warm liquid slide down my throat. I looked up to him as he smiled, and he grabbed my face, kissing me.

"Oh baby, that was amazing, I fucking love how I taste on your beautiful lips." I kissed him back and he rolled me over to take me again, and again, until we were spent. *Who needs the gym when you have Mr. Sex on Legs giving you a non-stop cardio workout?*

I looked over to the window and watched the snow begin to fall. What a beautiful sight to take in. Living in the south, you really don't get the opportunity to experience a real winter. I just wanted to run outside and catch snowflakes on my tongue. Instead, I asked Walker, "Can you tell me what happened with your father?" He took in a deep breath, and told me no. I was surprised by his answer, but I didn't push him. We held each other for another hour or so, and then we both needed to get up for our classes. Freddy was already gone by the time we made our way in to the kitchen. Coffee was on the stove, bless his heart.

We walked hand in hand on the grounds of NYU, and felt the snow and ice under our feet. This was amazing. I couldn't wait to call Nana today to tell her about my first snow experience. That is, until I hit an ice patch and fell hard on my ass. Walker almost fell too, but he was quicker on his feet. "Stop laughing at me, you jerk, and help me up." Now my ass was wet, and I could feel the cold wetness through my gloves. "I'm sorry babe, but that was too funny and I needed that. Thanks for making my day."

"My pleasure, baby... Always happy to embarrass myself for you."

"No chance at that happening, Reese, I love you."

"I love you too. I have to get to class now, have a great day." We kissed and walked in opposite directions. I tried not to let it bother me that he didn't tell me about his father, and I held on to the hope that everything would be okay. After my classes, I went over to the Elite offices downtown to meet up with Marsha. She had me booked for my first cover; I couldn't contain my happiness over it. I was going to be on the cover of Cosmopolitan Magazine... *How did she manage to pull this off?* Marsha was an amazing agent. She always pushed for the best for her clients. Oh how lucky I was to be one of them.

"You are a hot ticket, my southern belle, and several designers are requesting you for their spring lines. Can you imagine, Reese? You can be modeling in Milan for fashion week. Are you excited, or what?"

I was beyond thrilled with the opportunity that I had been given. I hugged Marsha, and we went over my calendar for my upcoming shoots and shows. Most of my work was planned around my school schedule. Marsha tried hard to accomplish that. From the beginning, I was adamant about work not interfering with school, but we always seemed to make it work. As I looked over the December dates, I noticed that I was booked out the week of Christmas. That was the same week I planned on introducing Walker to my grandparents back home in Georgia.

"Marsha, I can't work on Christmas, and it's my birthday. I need to be home in Georgia, not halfway across the world."

"I'm sorry doll, but if you want this cover, then that's when it's happening." How was I going to explain this to my family, let alone Walker? He couldn't wait to meet my grandparents, and he wanted to ask my Granddaddy for his blessing to marry me.

"I'm sorry, Marsha, but I'm going to have to pass." I thought my agent was going to faint.

"Hell no, Reese! You just can't say no to *Cosmo*, and after all that I have arranged for you, it is too late to cancel or find a replacement. I would look like a laughing stock, and you don't want to hear what they would say about you. Whatever you have had planned will have to work around this shoot." Without allowing me to say another word, she clipped clopped off and called out, "See you on the plane."

I took my long taxi ride home, and all I could think about was how to tell him. I called Walker to meet me at my apartment. We arrived within only a few minutes from one another. He scooped me up in to his arms, and he sensed my tension. "What's wrong baby?" I held his hand, and we walked inside and closed the world out. I poured some wine for us so I could break the news to him.

"I'm afraid that our Christmas plans need to change. I don't want to cancel or miss out on anything with you or my family, but it's a work opportunity that can't be changed. I tried to work around it, but there's no way."

"What is it?" I looked up at him with a bewildered expression on my face. "The opportunity, Reese... what is it?"

"I will be on the May cover of Cosmopolitan Magazine, but the shoot has to take place the week of Christmas. It's in Milan."

Walker's reaction takes me completely by surprise. He kissed me and congratulated me. "We need to celebrate, how fantastic! I will buy every copy that hits the news stand!"

"Walker, what about Christmas? Aren't you upset that our plans are now changing?"

"We can work it out and still find the time to visit your family and celebrate your birthday. Let me see your schedule."

Walker and I looked over the schedule for over an hour with each of us writing plans out in our notebooks. We compromised, and came up with a different plan. We would take a long weekend over Thanksgiving to fly down to see my family and then have an early Christmas for the two of us. We were going to celebrate my 21st birthday when I returned right before New Year's. We hated to be apart from each other, but Walker never held me back from my modeling. He asked me if I still wanted to become a teacher, and I of course said, "Yes."

Modeling was never my first choice. I earned a nice paycheck from it. However, teaching was always my goal. Weeks flew by, and before we knew it, we were on a plane to Georgia. He never did tell me about his talk with his father, and I never brought it up again. All he did say is that he didn't want me to worry about anything and he would handle his father. I had no reason to believe that he wouldn't, but deep down I was still scared and I was just getting better at hiding my fears to Walker. I vowed to always be strong and not falter in my promise that I made to myself so many years ago. My mother chose a different path... I would not. I just had to remember that even when you're strong, sometimes it's also okay to be scared. Scared is not an emotion that should be defined as weak, it's natural.

In the short time that I'd been here in New York, my life had completely changed. Staring at myself in the mirror I saw myself, but the girl that left Georgia, was not the same girl anymore. I hope when I visit Nana and Granddaddy, I can learn to hold my tongue. I had developed quite the mouth living here, but I still knew my manners. I would always remain respectful when it came to my grandparents. Besides, Nana knew a few words of her own.

CHAPTER EIGHT

Coming together...

"ARE YOU NERVOUS?" I asked Walker as we walked hand in hand through the airport. He quietly shook his head no, but he couldn't hide his apprehension from me. "Walker, my grandparents are amazing people. You will love them and the town I grew up in." It felt so right being here. I couldn't wait to get a comforting hug from them. I had kept them in the dark about the threats Walker's father had made against me. I couldn't and wouldn't upset them, so I only mentioned the good stuff. Nana did have a sixth sense about people though, so she would have known if I was lying.

I would have liked to have seen the Macy's Thanksgiving Day Parade. It would have been my first time in person. However, Walker insisted that we come to Georgia for Thanksgiving considering we will be on separate continents for Christmas. *Yeah, that's another thing Nana doesn't know yet. Ugh... please let her be happy for me.*

As we drove through Pottersville, I pointed out all the historical landmarks to him. He was transfixed on the buildings. We turned the corner and I pointed to my grandparents' book depot and café. I almost wanted to stop the car and go in, but I knew they were back home waiting for us. "I love you, Walker. Thank you for coming home with me." He immediately kissed me, glided his hand over my thigh, and gently squeezed it.

"Thank you, Reese. This is a big step, and I'm so happy that I'm here with you."

"Well no turning back now, because we're here." I had asked the driver to beep the horn when we arrived, but they were already waiting for us on the porch. Granddaddy came down and opened up my door. I walked right in to his arms. *I missed this man so much. I needed him more than he knew.* Nana was next greeting us. She looked so beautiful, but loaded with flour all over her. I knew she was probably on a baking frenzy, and when we hugged I smelled cinnamon on her. *Oh my favorite, apple pie.*

I held each of their hands and introduced Walker to them. He was beaming at me, and Nana was smiling back at him, while Granddaddy eyed him before extending his hand. *Oh bless his heart.* "Granddaddy, this is my boyfriend, Walker Reed."

"It's a pleasure to meet you son, and welcome to our home."

"Thank you, sir. It's great to be here and share the holiday with you." Nana took my hand, so I could I follow her into the house. The house looked the same and nothing had changed. It had only been a few months since I left for school, but I didn't know how much I missed home until I found myself here again. Every wall was covered with family pictures. Nana always had a camera handy. The one picture I kept with me back in New York hung above the fireplace, but only in a bigger size. Walker put his hands around my shoulders and held me as I was lost in the picture. My eyes were glassy, and I was on the verge of crying. I had to excuse myself and went upstairs to my old room.

Nana had joked that she was going to turn it in to a work-out room, yeah right! I opened the door to see all my boxes were stored. My queen sized bed was layered with my favorite quilt that I had sewn with my mother. Fresh flowers were on my side table, and a welcome home basket was filled with my favorite treats from the café. The sobs came softly and quietly. I let them all out until I had no tears left. I felt him watching me, but he gave me the space that I needed. Walker only joined me when I held my hand out to him. Kissing away my tears, he promised me that he would do everything in his power to never see me cry again. I felt drained. When he was next to me, the excitement built up inside of me. All I wanted to do was make love to him… doubtful while under my grandparents roof, but I had a few secret places that I planned on taking Walker to. Once I knew Granddaddy was asleep, with his shotgun safely stowed, I would take Walker out to explore the property.

I wasn't ready to talk to my grandparents yet, especially after my moment of sadness. Walker had told Nana that I was going to take a nap to clear my head. While I remained upstairs, he got to know them better and even helped Nana with dinner. I joined them about an hour later when all was ready. We joined hands in prayer as Granddaddy began to say grace. This was something unfamiliar to Walker. He bowed his head anyway and listened as my Granddaddy spoke on how thankful he was for his family, and all that God had bestowed on us. I kept smiling at him while we enjoyed the delicious home cooked meal that Nana had prepared for us. I quietly watched my boyfriend talk with my grandparents, laugh at Granddaddy's jokes, and savor every last bite of Nana's apple pie. My heart swelled with love for him. If only his family could be more accepting of me… then everything would be perfect.

Nana always had said to me, "You can't please everyone that comes in and out of your life. You always have to be your best self, and if that's not good enough, then that person is not worthy of you." *Oh, I wanted to believe her words, but this was Walker's father. If we ever got married, then he would be my family too.*

I helped Nana clean up while Walker and Granddaddy had a chat on the porch. I joined them a little while later to find them both laughing. I let out a sigh of relief and sat down on my boyfriend's lap while he wrapped his arms around me. Granddaddy said his goodnights, and with a kiss to my head he was off to bed. "So how are you? Did Granddaddy ask you a million and one questions?"

Holding me tighter, Walker looked up in to my eyes and said, "I love you, Reese Mitchell, and yes he asked me many questions. However, there was only one that I asked him."

"What question was that, Walker?" was all I could manage to say to him. He looked so relaxed. All I saw when he looked back at me was love.

"I asked for your hand in marriage, requesting your grandfather's permission to do so." I gasped. "He gave me his blessing, Reese. Although I don't have a ring with me now, I plan on presenting one to you in the near future, so be ready my love."

"Walker, I love you so much, but we still have to learn more about one another. I have many things that I haven't even shared with you."

"Reese, I know everything I need to know about you, *please...* stop worrying. Once we graduate in a few months, we will have the rest of our lives to be happy and take on the ride of our lives just loving each other. Reese, you are my forever."

I hugged him back with every fiber of my being. I kept telling him how much I loved him back. I told him that I was his "forever," and my answer was yes... when he was ready to officially ask me, that is! I led Walker away from the house and through the field of flowers that led to an open patch of land. The stars were so bright tonight, and the moon was beaming down on us. We stretched out in each other's arms and gazed up at the night sky. We talked so much about our relationship, our plans for the future, and my fears were finally gone. I couldn't wait any longer, and I lunged myself at him.

"Make love to me, Walker... right here... right now." I didn't have to ask him twice. He slowly began to remove my clothing and take me under the stars. Tonight our lovemaking was different from all of our other times; this felt like we were sealing our souls together. Consummating all of the promises we had made to one another. My fears had been erased along with the doubt. *It was me and Walker against the world.* He made me believe we could handle anything life would challenge us with, even the great Phillip Reed.

Our Thanksgiving holiday was coming to a close, but there was one place that I needed to visit before heading back to New York. Nana had asked me if I needed her to come with me. I had Walker though, and I needed to introduce him to my parents. Walker and I carried two bouquets of flowers for each of their graves. Mama always loved wild flowers in an array of colors. My dad always liked roses because it was the one flower he said was the universal connection to a woman's heart. I always laughed after I heard that because Granddaddy says the same thing. I knelt down before them, began talking, and tried very hard not to cry. I can never repay my grandparents for taking care of me after my parents died, after all they sacrificed for me. But deep down I was still so angry. I was angry at the truck driver that killed my father. I was angry at my mother for being weak and giving up. They both left me, but most of all I was angry with God for calling them home. They should have been with me.

What did I know back then? I was a scared ten year old without her Mama and Daddy. The ghosts still lingered from time to time. I told my parents about Walker and how much I loved him. He held my hand the entire time. I told them that I hoped they were happy for me, and when it comes to the day that I do marry the man I love, they would send me a sign that they are watching from the heavens to wish us well. Walker held me in his arms while he kissed me gently, watching for tears that never fell.

I was already so much stronger thanks to Walker. He made me better, made me believe that I could be happy and not let the past define me. He was amazing. I often wondered why he was not like Phillip, but I saw his mother's kindness in him. We said our goodbyes to my grandparents as we left for our trip home. Our flight was delayed a bit due to storms up the East Coast. Finally, and exhausted, we arrived in New York after midnight. We went back to Walker's apartment instead of mine. It was Sunday, so I had all day to do my laundry, catch up with Freddy, and get ready for classes on Monday.

CHAPTER NINE

Missing you...

THE WEEKS THAT followed our mini vacation to Georgia were extremely chaotic. Our semesters ended, and the holidays were upon us. Walker was traveling with his father back and forth to California to oversee how their new offices were coming along. I was in Italy shooting my Cosmopolitan cover. Although Freddy hadn't officially moved to Milan yet, he already had an apartment rented and furnished by the time I arrived in the city. He had left New York before me, only taking his personal items that he couldn't live without along with a small garment bag. I didn't know at the time that he had sent some boxes over already. The rest that he had in New York, his uncle would retrieve.

My heart was missing my best friend and my boyfriend. Thinking to myself as I looked around the fast paced studio with all of the photographers shouting out commands to the models, *is this what I really wanted to do with my life?* My dream was to become a teacher. I loved the arts, and I wanted to inspire children. Modeling had been good for me, but I was feeling out of place. My relationship with Freddy had changed. He told me that I was looking into things that weren't there, but I knew better. If I wasn't sure then, seeing what is happening right before my eyes convinced me that Freddy was here to stay and I was not.

I went through hair and make-up, ten costume changes, and then my photo shoot was over. Eleven hours of smiling, being robotic for the camera, and I was exhausted. Marsha, my agent, was on cloud nine. They all invited me out on the town, and I didn't want to be the odd person out. So, I joined Freddy, Marsha, and a few of the other models that I had met today. They dragged me all over the city to the hottest clubs where Freddy and the others danced the night away. I didn't get back to my hotel room until four a.m. I was gone for a whole twenty-four hours without checking in with Walker. My phone was completely dead.

After I got up to my room I phoned the concierge for any missed calls or messages. He sent a bell hop up with an envelope full of them, and I counted more than ten messages. I also listened to a very angry Walker on my voicemail.

"Reese, what the fuck is going on over there? I have called and called you, where are you? I am trying to be calm, but my patience has run out, and I am about to board a plane to bring you home. To be away from you is hard enough, but now you are not calling me when you said you would? I don't care what the clock says. When you get this message along with the others that I have left, CALL ME!"

My heart plummeted with listening to him on my phone. I dialed his number with shaky fingers, and he answered on the second ring. "Reese, is that you?"

"Hi," I squeaked out. I didn't want to argue with him, especially with me being so far away, but I prepared myself for the worst.

"Thank god you are okay. Why haven't you returned my calls? I have been so worried about you. Talk to me baby, what is going on?"

"Walker, I'm fine, believe me. I'm so sorry that I worried you. Had I known you left all these messages at the hotel, I would have called you sooner. My phone had died, and I just received them now."

"What time is it now in Milan?" he asked while the tone of his voice had changed from worry to angry again.

"It's four thirty a.m."

"Are you just getting back to your hotel now? Where the hell have you been all night, Reese? Who were you out with?"

"Walker, if you think I would cheat on you, then you are crazy! I did an eleven hour photo shoot, and I was invited out by Freddy along with some members of the crew when we were done shooting. Yes, I just got back now to my hotel room. All I did was spend some time with friends... nothing happened." After a long silent pause I asked him, "Walker, are you still there?"

"I have to go, Reese. I will see you when you get back to New York." The line went dead, and so did my heart.

What just happened here? Why was he angry with me? I know I should have called him. After I explained what happened, I was hop-ing he would have understood and accept my apology. God! I hate this place and I want to just go home.

I took a shower and then slept for a few hours. I had missed the luncheon that I was supposed to attend. Marsha was flipping out, but I explained that I wasn't feeling well. I wasn't lying; my heart ached, and my stomach was nauseous. I was ready to finally go to sleep, when there was persistent knocking at the door.

In a huff, I pulled opened the door to find Freddy leaning up against the wall outside of my room. "Can I come in?"

I stepped aside and gestured with my hand for him to come in. Wrapping my robe tightly around my waist, we sat down and talked. It was long overdue, and I let him go first. "Sorry I woke you up, Peaches. You look like hell."

"Gee, thank you friend, just what I needed to hear. If you must know, this is the broken hearted look when your boyfriend dumps you."

"What? You and Walker? Over?"

Sighing and shaking my head, I said, "I don't know, Freddy, he was really upset with me that I didn't keep in better contact with him. We argued, and although I apologized, he was distant. He said he would see me back in New York."

"I'm sorry, Peaches. I feel like this is my fault in a way. I pressured you to take this job. I ignored you for days. I had Marsha coerce you into going out with us, even when I knew you were tired. I don't think it's over for you and Walker. Your man called me to tell my ass off."

"What did you just say?"

"I think you heard me the first time. Walker phoned me and asked me what was going on here in Milan. I told him the truth: that I wasn't being a great friend because I was too caught up in my own shit to pay attention to you. I was kind of out of it when he called. I may have mentioned that you went home with one of the male models, but then forgot that Antonio was gay, so I told him not to worry."

No, No, No! Oh my god, this can't be happening. "Freddy, how could you say that to Walker, of all people? He is completely jealous, and can be downright obsessive when it comes to me. He doesn't take too kindly to my modeling as it is, but also doesn't stand in my way either. Now I understand why he was so cold to me when I called him. I have to fix this, Freddy. Right now!"

"Calm down Reese… I already talked to him. I sobered up and called him to explain everything. He's much calmer now, and no one is breaking up with anyone. Your hot man only has eyes for you. He isn't going anywhere, Reese. I'm sorry I've been a shitty friend. Can we talk? Really talk and clear the air between us?"

I answered Freddy with a hug. We talked all day…just like our college days down south. We looked at the clock and saw that hours had passed. I quickly got dressed, and my best friend and I spent the rest of our time exploring the beautiful city together and catching up. Whatever Walker wanted to say to me would have to wait until I got back to New York.

Freddy did confirm that he wasn't returning home with me, and I would be on my own. I already knew this in my heart, but hearing it didn't make me feel any better. I would always love Freddy, we have shared so much together, but our lives were going in different directions. It was time to watch him fulfill his dreams. We promised to stay in touch, but you know how that goes. I only hoped it wouldn't be true for us.

Marsha and I said our goodbyes to each other in London. She would be returning to New York at the end of January. She decided to take an extended holiday and told me how happy she was that I was her client. The editors over at Cosmopolitan were thrilled with my pictures and expressed interest on working with me in the future. My mind was all over the place and I couldn't make any decisions right now. Marsha had lined up work for me through spring and summer if I wanted the work. I would give her my answer on all of it when she returned home.

I hadn't had any other communication with Walker since our fight, only a text or two telling him my flight itinerary. It was freezing, and I was shivering as I walked in to my darkened apartment, minus one best friend. Leaving my bags where I dropped them, I walked into my living room to find wall to wall flowers all arranged perfectly throughout the room. Holding my hand over my heart I said, "What the?"

There he stood, my beautiful man holding one long stemmed red rose. I blinked a few times and tried to catch my breath with what he had done. Clearly we weren't over; if anything we were about to make up.

Walking slowly over to where I was standing, he embraced me with wanton desire and passion. He breathed me in, as I closed my eyes and thanked God that he was here. "I'm so sorry for not trusting you. It made me crazy being without you. Please forgive me, Reese?" He began to slowly mark my neck with soft kisses, and marking me with his delicious tongue. Holding my face in his hands and looking directly into my eyes, he whispered…"Forgive me"

Walker had a way of using his body to answer for him and for us. It was our private expression on how to communicate with one another.

I took his hand, and led him to my bedroom. I found more roses strewn out all over the room. I backed him up until his legs hit my bed, making him fall backwards on to the mattress. I climbed on top of him, began kissing him, trailing my tongue down his throat and moving my hands under his shirt. He let out a savage groan and flipped me on to my back. Walker was quick and had my blouse off of me before I could blink. My bra and skirt were next, leaving me only in my panties. Softly touching my breasts with his masculine hands he began moving down my neck with whispers of kisses. His kisses become more passionate as he bit down on my nipples, making me cry out in pleasure.

He didn't stop as his hand traveled down toward my weeping sex. He ripped my panties from my body and tenderly slid his fingers over my clit. Kneeling between my legs he continued his sensual assault on my body. My eyes rolled back as his soft kisses made their way down my torso and finally entered my pussy. My body was writhing under him, and I could not control the noises coming out of my mouth. My hands found his head, and I pulled him further down into me until I could take no more. I screamed out his name. As my body was convulsing, he used his forehead to put pressure right above my pelvis, and my orgasm lasted longer than any other. He lifted his head, and with one more flick of his dexterous tongue, I came again. Not letting my buzz wear off, he flipped me onto my stomach to take me from behind.

I was on my knees with my ass in the air; he spanked me twice as he pounded me... hard. My walls clenched around him as he pushed harder and faster until we came together, with him emptying himself into me. He collapsed on my back, our fingers entwined, as he kissed my neck. "I love you, Reese Mitchell, and if you didn't know it before...You. Are. Mine. Forever."

Oh holy hell! "Yes, I do know that, Walker, but thank you for the reminder." I was spent, and we just fell asleep holding each other. Hours later I woke to him inside of me again. Three orgasms later, we were sitting cross-legged facing each other and eating dinner out of Chinese food containers. *Was it dinner? I lost track of time.*

"I love the flowers, thank you."

"You deserve them and so much more. I should have never doubted you while you were away. These feelings that I'm experiencing are so new, and ones that I have never felt before. They took me by surprise, and I really didn't know what to do with them. My father also didn't help my missing you. Not to darken our day, but the entire time we were in California, all he talked about was Elizabeth. That she would be the perfect choice to decorate the offices, and she would be an asset to the company."

"Is that was Elizabeth does? Is she an interior designer?" I asked with curiosity. We haven't talked about Elizabeth in months. I almost forgot about her.

"Her father, Henry, is also in real estate, and she has just earned her designing degree. Elizabeth just has a natural instinct about these things, and has assisted both her parents in many of their projects. My father insists that she is my match, but I keep telling him to stop. Elizabeth and I are nothing more than friends. I'm completely in love with this southern belle from Georgia. Now, she's a looker. She is breathtaking, and her legs… don't even get me started."

I throw a fortune cookie at him, he has me laughing so much to the point that I'm in tears. We crack open the cookie and it reads…

YOU & ME = FOREVER…

CHAPTER TEN

Why?

"DID YOU DO this? I laugh as I read the fortune again."

My man smiled back at me and raised his hands up as if he was surrendering to me. "Not me babe, must be fate, and fate wanted us to get this fortune." *How can I argue with the universe, when it gave me Walker?*

Kissing him back, I whispered... "Yes, baby, its fate."

"We have to get ready for my father's party. I have everything I need here, so we can just call for the car when we are ready."

"Walker, I want to spend New Year's Eve with you, but your father...not so much. He scares the hell out of me. We already know he doesn't like me. If I show up on your arm it's just going to put more fuel on the fire. He clearly does not want me with you. While we were apart, I gave it some thought. I can't make him like me, but I will not have him disrespect me any longer. So, I would rather not have any unwanted confrontations with him if I could help it. Please do not ask me to go."

"Reese, my father can go to hell. I don't care what he wants, because he doesn't get to decide who I end up with. So fuck him and his plans for my future. He can't hurt us, Reese. He can't take my inheritance away from me. All of that is locked up and safely set up for me in a trust, and it becomes all mine the day I graduate college. My grandfather made sure that I would take my rightful place in the company; I have known this since I was young. I have been groomed to take it over one day from him, just as it was Phillip who succeeded his. I'm not worried about his threats, and you shouldn't be either. I will fire his ass if I have to, but please don't let him get to you."

"Will Elizabeth be there tonight?" I couldn't help the vehemence of my tone when I mentioned her name. I was downright jealous of her, and she never did anything to me except love Walker herself.

"Yes, she will be there tonight along with her parents. I told you how close they are to my family, but again you have no worries when it comes to Elizabeth. Now please, let's drop this. Let's have another round while we are in the shower."

He was dressed in a black Armani Tux, while I was wearing a Ralph Lauren gown. It was given to me while I was in Italy. A present from the man himself, and he expressed how happy he was that I was the model that made his design come to life. I was completely taken back by his compliments. Having only been in this business for a short time, I was definitely going to enjoy the perks.

"You are stunning. Turn around for me." I turned around for Walker, until he stopped me. He looked me up and down and shook his head. "I don't know, Reese, there's something missing...hmmm."

Without me catching on, he presented me with a Tiffany's box. I covered my mouth and began to cry. "Reese, you don't even know what it is yet, crying comes later." Now I know he was teasing me. We had exchanged our Christmas gifts weeks ago before the holiday. We didn't want to miss out due to all of our traveling.

"This gift is different," Walker explained. "Reese, what's in this box you already have. This gift symbolizes our love, and it represents our future. Wear this with the knowledge that you will always have me right where I belong." He slowly opened the box, and my eyes brightened with the site of a gorgeous platinum locket with an encrusted diamond heart shining back at me. It was the most beautiful locket I had ever seen. I opened it: one side contained a picture of us that was taken back in Georgia, and the other one was of Walker. He told me that as time goes on, we can change the pictures to our wedding photo, and then to our children. He asked me to turn it over and read the inscription. It simply read…*You are my forever. Love, Walker.*

"It's beautiful, baby. Thank you so much for the best gift I have ever received." I kissed him, and he used his thumb to stop my falling tears.

"This is only the beginning for us, Reese. We will have all the time in the world. If you ever doubt it, just look to your locket, and know you are holding my heart." He placed the necklace on me, and I vowed to never take it off.

Our car pulled up to the front of the Reed's apartment building. Photographers lined the sidewalk trying to catch a glimpse of who was behind the tinted windows. Holding my hand, Walker turned to me. "Are you ready, beautiful?"

I take a deep breath and answer him, "Yes."

I'm told that the Reed's New Year's Eve party was one that was never to be missed, especially from New York's finest families. I was no stranger to the cameras, but this felt all too surreal for a holiday party. We quickly made our way into the building, to the safety of the private elevator. A few reporters shouted out and asked Walker who was his escort of the evening. One reporter asked him who was escorting Elizabeth. I found that very strange because Walker had always told me they were friends only.

"It's me and you against the world, right, baby? I love you… let's roll." Hand in hand we made our entrance into the beautifully decorated great room. It had vaulted ceilings with fine artwork that lined the walls. Walker's mother greeted us first. She looked beautiful in her emerald green gown. She was wearing matching jewels that decorated her neck, wrists, and ears.

"Oh my darling son, Happy New Year. Hello to you too, dear."

"Happy New Year, Mrs. Reed. You look lovely, and thank you

for having me here tonight."

"Oh don't give it a second thought dear, enjoy yourself." Two air kisses later and she was off mingling with the crowd. I eyed the other guests, and my eyes found his father staring back at me. Phillip Reed was surrounded by a group of men drinking what looked like scotch. He raised his glass at me, then continued on with his conversation. I felt chills run down my spine there was such darkness in his eyes. "How can a woman like Olivia be married to a man like that?" I asked Walker that very question after meeting his father. He explained that his father is very different from his alter ego that he often shows to the world. "When Phillip Reed is with his wife, and her alone, he is a man in love." It was so confusing to believe that. All I have seen of this man is a controlling, ruthless jerk that shows more hate than love.

Walker and I danced with only each other until we were interrupted by Elizabeth and his father. Elizabeth looked gorgeous, and her smile was genuine, unlike Phillip who just sneered at me through his fake smile. Phillip asked if he could share a dance with me, while Elizabeth danced with Walker. Walker was hesitant at first, but then I winked at him. I meant what I promised myself. *Phillip Reed was not going to intimidate or disrespect me.*

"Having a good time Ms. Mitchell?" He gripped my hand with his other holding steady at the small of my back.

"I am Mr. Reed, thank you." I kept my answers simple.

"I believe I asked you to end things with my son, and yet here you are at my party. For a smart girl, you really don't take direction well. That's a pity, my dear, because now you have forced my hand."

"Mr. Reed, why are you doing this to me? I've done nothing wrong, but love your son and he loves me. Please just let us be. I promise not to mention this to him."

"You can do whatever you want, Ms. Mitchell, because after I share my knowledge of your past with him, he will be so disgusted that he will leave you. I was trying to actually help you, but you defy me. So you are leaving me with no choice."

I felt sickened by his threats. He gripped my hand tighter as I tried to pull away from him. I glanced over to Walker, who was dancing and having a conversation with Elizabeth, they were both smiling at each other.

"You see that my dear? She is his match. Not you. And the sooner you realize this, the better off you will be. The longer you wait and continue to ignore my warnings, then you truly will only have yourself to blame. This is your last chance... Remember that, Ms. Mitchell." He released me and turned away as if threatening to destroy one's happiness was no big deal. *I have to get out of here and I have to leave now.* Walker is still dancing with Elizabeth with his back to me.

I quickly walked to the coat closet to retrieve my wrap. I ran for the elevators, and as the doors began to close, Walker called for me. He was too late, the doors were closing. A waiting cab was at the curb, and I jumped in. I shouted my address, and he hit the gas. Walker was going to be out of his mind with worry, but I couldn't even begin to explain this to him. *His father is evil! He is probably telling Walker right now about me, the part of my past that I didn't share with him yet.*

Where the hell was I going to go? I shouldn't go back to my apartment. He will find me there. Freddy is not here, and the few friends I do have are out of town celebrating the New Year. I have no choice, I have nowhere else to go. I should be with the man I love right now, and instead I did exactly what Phillip wanted me to do...I left Walker.

I locked my door behind me, and if Walker showed up, he could use the key that I gave him. *I am drained, and I don't have the slightest idea on how to handle this. His father made it perfectly clear tonight that if I don't yield to his wishes, I somehow will suffer for it, but how? This man is not God? He doesn't have the power to just fuck with people's lives. I'm such an idiot! Why did I leave the party? I should have slapped his face, and spit at him. That rotten, bastard hiding behind those fake smiles... while he is hating me and plotting my demise. I don't understand this at all. I'm simply in love with his son, and Walker loves me. He has proved it to me over and over again. I must look like a crazy person to him.*

It was after midnight, and I was just lying in bed when I glanced at my phone. *Where is he? Why isn't he here?* I realized that I'm still wearing my gown, and it had been hours since I had come home. I forced myself to get up and go into the bathroom to wash my face and change. I put on one of Walker's NYU sweatshirts that he had left here. It smelled like him. I breathed in his scent and committed it to memory. I'm surrounded by the beautiful roses that are all around my apartment. Reuniting with him yesterday was the happiest moment of my life. My hand slowly slid to my neck and touched my locket. I open it up and remember his heartfelt words that he recited to me. ***You are my forever. Love, Walker.***

I missed celebrating our first New Year's together. My mind was replaying the dance I shared with Phillip, and how once again he threatened me. I had no clue as to where Walker could have been. I continued to sit there in my darkened room, praying he would come home to me. I must have fallen asleep, because I didn't hear him when he finally arrived.

"Reese, baby... are you here?" My door slowly creaked open, and he turned the side light on. I looked up to find Walker standing over me. My pillowcase was soaked with tears, my make-up had run down my face, and my eyes hurt.

"Baby, are you okay? My father said you suddenly fell ill and needed to leave. I would have been here sooner, but my mother slipped and hurt her ankle. She didn't want to go the hospital so I waited with her until our family physician showed up to tend to her."

"Is she okay, your mother?"

"Yes, she's fine. Just a bad sprain. She has to take it easy for a few days, but nothing's broken."

"I'm more concerned about you at the moment. Can I get you anything? Soup perhaps?" He was totally in the dark as to why I left, and he looked so worried because he thought that I was sick. I must have looked awful with all the crying that I'd done since I left the party.

"Walker, I'm not sick. Don't you think I would've told you if I felt sick? Your father lied to you. He's the reason why I left the party."

"What are you talking about? Please tell me what the hell is going on with you and my father." He shrugged off his coat and tuxedo jacket and sat beside me. I sat up and reached for my glass of water, taking a few sips to calm myself down. This was not how I envisioned my New Year with Walker, but his father had left me no choice.

"Do you love me, Walker?"

"What kind of question is that Reese? Of course I love you, more than life itself. You're wearing my heart, remember?"

"Yes, I remember. Walker, I love you so much that it hurts, but you need to know something before we take one more step in our relationship." I raise my hand to his lips and stop him from speaking.

This would have been hard enough having to explain my past to him, but now his own father has tried to use it against me. "A few years ago when I first began to model, I, along with several other girls, had our pictures used for what we later found out to be porn. The pictures were used without our knowledge, and they began circulating throughout several porn sites. The photographer that did this was acting alone and was immediately fired by the well-known agency he had worked for. We sued him, the company that bought the pictures, the company he worked for, and we won our lawsuit. We shut down the distribution of the movie and to my knowledge everything was removed from being online."

"This happened during my junior year while I attended GSU. I was humiliated and ashamed. My life as I knew it had changed, and that's when I made the decision to leave Georgia to start over in New York. Your father led me to believe that he knows of this and threatened to tell you himself. I guess if he made me out to be a whore, and obviously had the pictures to prove it, then why would his son ever be with a girl like me?" I stopped talking to wipe away my falling tears.

There…I said it. And now that asshole Phillip can't hold this above my head anymore. I let out the breath that I was holding and waited for Walker to react.

"Come here, baby." His eyes were glazed over as he took me in his arms and held me. "I'm so sorry that I didn't protect you tonight. My father is not going to get away with this, Reese. I promise. I will make this right for you, and for us."

"What about the photos, Walker? What if they get out and embarrass you?"

"Reese, I don't give a fuck about those pictures. Is this what you have been trying to tell me about your past? I know the beautiful girl in those pictures, and I know she would never do something like that. I love you, baby, and there's nothing about you that will ever embarrass me. I want to believe that the girl I love believes me when I say this to her. I have done everything to prove to you how much, Reese, and now it's your turn to prove it to me."

What the hell? "How, Walker? What can I say or do to make you believe me?"

"Don't run, Reese. It's that simple…Don't run. Stay with me. Trust that when I told you that you have my heart, just believe me, and we'll be okay."

Walker stripped out of his clothes and held me for the rest of the night. I'd never felt more safe than right there in his arms. He asked me to trust him, and I did. His father still scared me. However, with Walker by my side I felt stronger.

"Come on, baby, time to wake up." I rolled over to see Walker, and he was already dressed.

"What time is it?" I rubbed my eyes that are still sore from crying last night.

"It's a few minutes past nine, I want you to get in the shower and get ready. We are meeting my father in an hour."

"You can meet you father in an hour, I'll stay here under my covers." Walker came over and lifted my comforter and blanket up and then quickly threw them aside.

He then slid his arm under me and carried me to the bathroom. "Put me down, Walker, this is crazy. What are you doing?"

"Reese, if I have to, I will wash you myself, dress you, and drag you out of here. You will come with me. This bullshit with my father ends today, and after that, we will celebrate our do-over for New Year's. I am done with this man trying to screw with my life, and you are a part of it. So, are we going to argue some more, or are you going to get ready?"

I turned on the hot water in the shower and then leaned in to kiss him. *God, I wanted to have sex with him right now! This no-nonsense-in-your-face attitude was turning me on like you wouldn't believe, and I could almost see his hard on through his jeans.* Anytime we would fight, it would always lead to us fucking in a hot and aggressive manner. I slowly began to work my way down my legs when the curtain tore open, and his fiery eyes met mine.

"Don't you even think about touching yourself. I want all your pleasure, and later you will give it to me." Walker pulled my wet body, slammed me into his chest, and he kissed and sucked at my tongue. I think I came right there, but I certainly didn't tell him. *It's not as if I could hide any of my body's reactions from him...anymore.*

"Ready?" he asked me as we exited our car; this is the same question he asked me last night, but today, it had a whole new meaning. His parents were hosting brunch at their penthouse. A few close friends would be in attendance, along with Elizabeth and her family. We didn't wait to be announced as Walker led me in to the great room to call out to his father.

Elizabeth joined us first and looked worried. "What's wrong, Walker? Are you okay?" She touched his arm when she asked him, completely ignoring me.

"I'm fine, Elizabeth. Where is my father?" He asked through gritted teeth. She told us that his parents and guests were in the dining hall. Still holding my hand, he dragged me along with him, as he continued to call out for his father. Slamming the doors open and almost taking out the poor waiter, Walker pointed directly at his father. "We can do this in front of your guests, or you can join us in your study. Your choice, father. What will it be?"

His father, wiping his mouth with his linen napkin, simply placed it down and crossed his arms over his chest. "Walker, if you want to cause a scene in front of your mother and all of our friends, then you go right ahead, I have nothing to hide." *Oh he is good, smirking at me the entire time.*

He waited for Walker to explode. Walker turned to his mother and apologized for what he was about to do. She was the last person he wanted to hurt, but he needed to have his say. "You… My father, have meddled in my life for the last time. You will mind your own fucking business when it comes to my personal affairs. Ladies and gentlemen, if you didn't get the pleasure of meeting my beautiful girlfriend last night, then let me introduce her to you now. This is Reese Mitchell, and she will be Reese Mitchell Reed sometime in the near future. I love this woman with all of my heart and soul. She is my whole world. Phillip Reed over there, my devoted father, has been trying to threaten her, bully her, and extricate her from my life. I am here to tell you that he has failed in his attempts, and I will not allow this to continue for one more second."

He left my side, and walked right over to where his father sat, and leaned in to look directly into his eyes. "Stop fucking with me, father, and stay the hell out of my life. You want to come at me, fine you go right ahead, but don't go through my woman to get to me, ever again!"

He turned to Elizabeth, and gave her a hug. "I'm sorry, friend, but whatever my father has promised you is simply not true. I love Reese, and my future is with her. I'm sorry if this hurts you… I truly am."

All eyes were on me, as Walker re-joined me at the foot of the table. His mother was crying, and Elizabeth was soon about to join her. He gripped my face and kissed me hard in front of his family and guests. "I love you, baby. It's me and you against the world, right?" I nodded my answer, he grabbed my hand, and we never looked back.

Walker was shaking. He was so angry. I felt like I could throw up at any moment; it took every level of control to hold my stomach at bay. We drove back to his apartment in silence. I'd calmed down and so had my stomach. We entered his apartment, and he took my coat. He started a fire and invited me to join him. "Are you okay baby?"

"Oh Walker, how can you ask me that after all that you did today with your family...? How are you?"

"I'm free, Reese, and I have you. Fuck him and his bullshit. I meant every word that I said back there. I love you, I will marry you, and we will have our future. All you have to do is believe me, and everything will be fine." *Of course I believe him.*

We had our celebration do-over. We made love in front of the fire place. We just worshipped each other until we were completely sated. For the remainder of our holiday break, we stayed in between both of our apartments and locked out the rest of the world. Walker refused to speak with his father, and his mother was relentless on her attempts to talk to him.

The night before classes were to begin, I finally went home to do some of my massive pile of laundry and to my surprise, there was Freddy sitting on our couch. He was watching our favorite movie, "Pretty Woman."

"Freddy! Oh my goodness, what are you doing here?" I jumped into his arms, hugged my best friend, and then cried my eyes out. *What was happening to me? I had mood swings from hell: sick one day, happy the next. Now the sight of my best friend had me all over the place.*

"Calm down, Peaches, if you check your probably dead cell phone, you will find many messages from me telling you about my arrival."

"I'm sorry, it's been crazy around here lately." I filled Freddy in on everything that was going on. He was visibly pissed off and wanted to kick Phillip Reed's ass. I assured him that Walker had already taken care of him and hopefully this was the end of his personal crusade against me. I had called Walker and told him that Freddy was home. He wished me a good night with my friend and told me that he would see me at school.

As tired as I was, I stayed up half the night telling Freddy everything that he had missed, and then I listened to all of his stories about Milan. He had become a completely independent designer with his own line. I was so incredibly proud of him, and I couldn't wait to model more of his clothes. He would only be in New York for a few weeks, then back to Milan, and then he said he would be in California. He would be working out of a studio that was part of the Ralph Lauren dynasty. It would give Freddy some west coast exposure. He couldn't wait to get started with designing his new line.

I told him about Walker's plans for us and how he wanted me to join him in California after we graduated. Marsha already had work lined up for me, and it was totally up to me on how much I wanted to take on. My best friend hugged me, and it felt like old times again.

CHAPTER ELEVEN

Unexpected surprise...

"COME ON, PEACHES, time to wake up. Thank you for not an-swering your cell phone. Now that I'm up at this ungodly hour, I'm not happy. Marsha keeps calling for you. Um...Reese? Are you okay?"

Freddy pushed in my bathroom door and found me hugging the toilet. I was so sick. I had been vomiting for the past five minutes. *What the hell? I never puke.*

Kneeling down beside me, Freddy swept up my long hair and held it for me while I continued to empty my stomach. "Oh, I feel awful...Are you okay, Freddy? We ate the same thing last night."

"I'm good, Peaches, but you, on the other hand, need to get back in to bed. No classes for you today, and no modeling."

"I can't, Freddy! Marsha is expecting me, and I can't just not show up."

"Are you forgetting she's still away on her holiday? I only said she was calling me on my cell for you, Reese. You need to get back in bed. I'll call Razor to let him know that you won't make it today."

"Razor? Come again?"

"The photographer, and he is amazing. But unfortunately you won't get to see him today, so go back to bed, now."

I tried to stand up and nearly collapsed back down. Freddy caught me, and carried me back to my bed and tucked me in. "I'm going to run out and get you some things. I want you to stay put and try to rest while I'm gone."

"Freddy, please call Walker for me? If I don't show up at school and not call him, he will be worried."

"I'll take care of it, Peaches, just please rest. I'll be back soon."

As soon as I closed my eyes, sleep took over, and I didn't wake until four hours later. I was dazed at first as I slowly opened my eyes to find Walker watching me. "Hey," I whispered.

"Hey, yourself. How are you feeling? I couldn't concentrate on anything today after Freddy called me. Can you sit up and try to drink something for me?" Walker sounded so worried, and it was making my stomach hurt even more.

I slowly tried to sit up and lean against the headboard. Walker handed me some juice while I tried to take some small sips. It felt so good going down my dry throat. I handed him back the glass and then clasped my hand over his. "Baby, I probably just have the flu or something, please don't worry."

"I can't help it, you really look sick." I sigh, and shrug my shoulders. If he was throwing up for hours, I'm sure my beautiful man wouldn't look so hot either.

"Reese, I have to go, and I hate to leave you like this. I have some work to catch up on and some errands to take care of. Will you be okay here for a while without me?"

"I'll be fine, and Freddy is here if I need anything."

"He's not Reese, that's why I'm struggling with this. I arrived when he was rushing out the door. His uncle was in a car accident, and Freddy had to meet him at the emergency room."

"Oh poor Freddy… I have to call him."

"No need for you to do that right now, he called me about an hour ago and his uncle is fine, just suffering from a mild case of whiplash. Freddy is with him now and is getting him settled for the night. He said he has to wait until his aunts arrive back home and then he'll come back here, but I don't know how long he will be."

"Walker, I'm a big girl. I'll be fine, please go and do whatever you have to do."

"I love you, babe. I'll be back as soon as I can." He kissed me sweetly on my cheek and promised to hurry back to me. I tried to eat some soup and crackers, but my stomach still rumbled. Thank goodness that the little I did eat, I was able to keep down. My strength was returning, so I took a bath and curled up with a book. I lost the entire day and almost night. I checked my clock, and it read ten o'clock. Neither Walker nor Freddy had returned yet. I had no texts or missed calls on my phone. I felt tired again. I went back to sleep, hoping I would wake in Walker's arms.

I rolled over to reach out for him, but his side of the bed was cold. I sat up quickly and scanned my bedroom. Walker never came back home last night. I hurried in to the kitchen, and no Freddy either. I did see a note on the counter from Freddy, though.

He came home late, only to leave at dawn. He would be downtown in the studio all day, if I wanted to stop by. I also spotted an envelope that had been messengered over by The Elite Agency that I worked for. It must have arrived yesterday. I opened it to find a handwritten note from Marsha.

Dear Reese,

Here is your travel schedule and complete itinerary for the next several months. As you can see, Elite has worked around your school schedule for the local assignments until you graduate in May, and then thereafter, you are to be in Europe. I will be back in New York by the week's end; I will call you and set up a lunch meeting with you where I expect your answer to all of these arrangements.

Ta Ta for now,
Marsha

My head was spinning, and I couldn't even begin to think about modeling right then. Walker wanted me to join him in California after we graduated and begin our new life out there. *How am I going to tell him that my work will take me to Europe for the summer instead of California with him? Will he be reasonable and understand my commitments, or question my loyalty to him and our relationship?* Clenching my stomach, I sprinted for my bathroom as the bile was rising up my throat. Lying on the cool tile helped relieve the heat that was radiating off my body. My mind drifted to my Nana; she would always sing to me when I was sick. *I'm so weak right now, just rooted to this floor.*

"Reese, are you home?" I heard Freddy calling for me, but I was still on my bathroom floor. "Oh my god, Peaches, what the hell is going on with you?" Freddy rushed in and picked me up off the floor and brought me back to my bed. "In all the time that I have known you, you've never been sick like this before. What can I do? Should I call a doctor for you?"

"It's probably just the flu like I said. It will pass, and I'll be fine." Freddy eyed me up and down with curious eyes. I smacked him away to stop staring at me.

"Reese, when was your last period?"

"Eww! Freddy, um…that's none of your business, and why do you care?" *Why was I bitching at him when all he's trying to do is help me?*

"Reese, I care because I think you might be pregnant." With only those few words, I felt my heart sink as I absorbed what Freddy had just said.

Shaking my head at him, I hastily replied, "No Freddy, you're wrong; I'm not pregnant. Walker and I used protection."

"Come on Reese, really? You never forgot even once?"

Holding my head and trying to remember, the realization hit me like a brick wall. *Was it the time we had the wall sex? Or after I told him about his father, we didn't use protection. We never even discussed it after the fact; we just fucked like savage animals that couldn't get enough of each other until we passed out.* It dawned on me entirely.

"Oh my god… Freddy, I could be pregnant. What the hell am I going to do? Walker is going to flip out, and I don't even want to know how his father will react… Nana and Granddaddy? How will I tell them?" I begin to hyperventilate until Freddy pat my shoulder and then rubbed it, shaking me out of my momentary focus on the idea of being pregnant.

"Reese, you need to calm down. Let's think about this rationally. First of all, your man is not going to flip out. He loves you, and it takes two to tango. No glove, no love. Obviously the one part of his body he should have been thinking with took a vacation, so this is his responsibility too. Secondly, fuck his father and his bullshit. As for your grandparents, they may be shocked at first, but they love you more. Once it wears off, they will be happy. You will be making them great grandparents. I say that's pretty amazing."

"I'm not ready to be a mom. Walker isn't ready to be a father. This baby could not have possibly have come at a worse time. We are still learning so much about one another, and he wants me to just pick up and leave New York. His father has caused me so much stress with him constantly threatening me. Freddy, I don't know which way is up, and you're leaving in a few days. Where will that leave me?"

"You are not alone Reese. You need to trust your man. He loves you. I can delay my trip for a few days. Let's get you to the doctor and confirm what this is before you worry for one more minute."

"Freddy, I can find out right now if I'm pregnant by just taking a box test. I would rather do that first. Can you go down to the pharmacy and pick one up for me?"

"I'll be back in fifteen." I never saw Freddy move so fast, but I had to know before I would even think of telling Walker… *Speaking of whom, where is he?*

"Hello," he answered his phone in a curt tone.

"Hi babe, where are you? I thought you would be home by now." I heard voices in the background, here and there. I heard Walker asking for some privacy.

"I'm so sorry, Reese. I'm in the office with my father and some of his lawyers. I thought this would have been done by now, but I still have some things to iron out. The next few days and probably through the weekend, I'll be tied up with this. The offices in California are ready and we'll be going through a transitioning phase from New York to the west coast."

"Walker, what about school? Should you be missing that much?"

"Reese, I have everything covered. My last course load is very light and, hell, I can graduate now if I wanted to, but I'll wait to do the traditional walk in May. Let me get through with what I have to do here and I'll call you as soon as I can. You know I hate being without you, but this is for our future, baby, and I can't wait to begin it with you. I love you, gorgeous."

"I love you…" The line clicked off, and I hung up. I hadn't decided on anything yet and Walker was acting as if I did. I hadn't had the opportunity to explain Europe yet, or the fact that I may be pregnant with his child. I had Marsha to deal with, who still awaited my answer. I felt as if I was being pulled in all these directions and just needed a moment to take a breath.

Freddy came back and waved the pregnancy test box at me. *Time to find out if I'm knocked up…*

Five minutes later that felt like an hour, Freddy held up the stick and gave me a half smile. "Congratulations mama, you're pregnant."

I instantly put my hand to my stomach and began to cry. Freddy folded me into his chest and rubbed my back in small circles. "Shh, don't cry, it's going to be okay. You will be an amazing mother, and he or she is going to be gorgeous."

"Freddy, I'm pregnant with Walker's child. I'm going to be a mother."

"Um…yes, I believe we covered that, Peaches. Do you want to lie down for a while? You are turning pale again."

"No. I'm fine, Freddy. More than fine, I'm happy. He loves me, Freddy. He has told me every day since we've been together. This baby is a blessing, and he will be happy. I just know it." I hugged my best friend and kept reassuring myself that all would be okay. *It just has to be.*

The next few days were hard on me. Not seeing Walker didn't help, but we talked twice a day. I just carried on with school and managed to work on a few jobs. I had visited a doctor in the city and began taking my pre-natal vitamins. I was about six weeks pregnant, and I pretty much narrowed it down when we conceived.

Although it was very cold, the walk home helped me clear my head. I turned back a few times and felt as if someone had been watching me, but this is New York, so I tried to shrug it off. Me and my crazy imagination made it home in time to see Freddy off. "I'm not going to cry, Mackelstein, so don't even give me that look."

"I wouldn't dare, and I am going to miss you more than anything in the world. Have you told him yet?"

I shook my head no. "You are the only one, Freddy, and of course my doctor. The timing is off, but finally tomorrow I'm going to dinner at his place. I promise I will tell him then."

"It will be fine, Peaches. I'll call you when I get settled, and you can tell me all about it."

I couldn't help but feel like this was goodbye for Freddy and I. I didn't want to let him go. *We've been closer again, but our lives are changing at a rapid speed. Who knows where we will be in the future?* The thought of it made my stomach hurt, and I didn't think Freddy would appreciate me getting sick on his beautiful new suit. "I love you, best friend. No matter where we are in this big wide world, please don't ever forget that." Freddy kissed my cheek and quickly entered his car. I knew he was struggling as much as I was.

I waved him off, and then let my held back tears flow and flow until I had none left. The apartment was so empty. Everything in here belonged to Freddy's family. Freddy had taken his personal belongings with him, and all that remained was the few mementos that belonged to me. My entire life was still packed in boxes back home in Georgia.

A short while later I had phoned Nana, and her voice warmed my heart. We talked for over an hour, catching up with everything in my life. Well, almost everything. She too had a secret portal to my thoughts, but I never shared my pregnancy news with her. I needed to tell Walker first.

Life was about to change for me. In a few months I would be graduating NYU with my degree in hand. I would give up modeling and marry Walker. He hadn't asked me yet, but I knew that's where we were headed. Now we had a baby to look forward to. *Yes, life was perfect, and tomorrow can't come soon enough. I will be back in the arms of the man that I love.*

I hurried home from school, scrubbed, plucked, and buffed as quickly as I could. My insides were ablaze with thoughts of Walker occupying my mind all day. It had been days since we'd been together. I had missed my boyfriend so much. I just wanted to lose myself in him and have him lose himself in me. I glanced in the mirror; I looked hot and ready for my man. He had sent a car to take me back to his apartment. I rang the doorbell, and there he stood, looking breathtakingly handsome with his eyes burning all for me.

"Get in here, you." Swept up into his arms, Walker wrapped himself around me, circling his tongue with mine, and letting out moans of pleasure as we kissed. "Oh how I have missed you, Reese. I need to get you naked right now."

"Walker, hold on…I need to tell you something first."

"Later, baby. Whatever it is, my answer is yes. I've waited too long to be with you, and I need to see you right now." He took me right there up against the door, my panties off with one rip. No condom I noticed, as Walker pounded into me, and I screamed out his name in pure ecstasy. Walker took no mercy on my body, it was a feeling that I couldn't get enough of. We made love over and over again, until he collapsed on me. We were in front of the fire place, holding each other, and our breaths slowly returned back to normal.

"I've missed you so much Reese. I will never be away from you again; my heart can't bear the distance or the ache that never seems to go away until we are joined together."

I tried to tell him about the baby, but he just stopped me with more of his kisses, and his talking of our future. I reminded myself that tomorrow was another day. I let him do as he wished tonight, and tomorrow I would tell him that he was going to be a father. I was his, and had been since the day I let him in my heart. He owned me, body and soul, a possession he couldn't live without. I had no doubts about us because we belonged together. This was what he had promised…"Forever," and I was so ready to say yes to him.

Sunshine peered through the floor-to-wall windows. It looked like a beautiful day, as I rolled over to find a note and a flower on Walker's pillow.

Good Morning Baby,
You looked gloriously beautiful naked and sated. I couldn't bear waking you. Something has come up that needs my attention, but I will be back as soon as I can. I'm bringing you back your favorite breakfast: pastries, coffee, and of course the main entrée, me. Keep our bed warm for me.
Love, Walker

"Our bed"… the sound of that sends thrills through me. Yes our bed, hurry home my love, so I can show you how much I love you.

CHAPTER TWELVE

You will always be in my heart...

"WALKER!" I CALLED out to him, but realized he's not back yet. I drifted back to my contented sleep until the sound of the constant ringing of the doorbell woke me out of my slumber. Whoever it was would not take a hint. Wrapping myself up with a sheet with my robe nowhere to be seen, I hurried to the door thinking it's Walker who had forgotten his key. "You're back!" I exclaim, and my eyes look up to not Walker, but his father Phillip and his lawyer who I had met before.

I wrapped the sheet tighter around my flushed body, as the two men just strode in past me. They didn't even wait for me to say a word. "Hello, Ms. Mitchell," his father coldly hissed at me.

"Hello, Mr. Reed. Walker is not here at the moment."

"Yes, I know, Ms. Mitchell. You are the one I have come to see. Please get dressed and meet me in the living room, now." I simply nodded at him and ran back to the safety of Walker's bedroom. *What the hell is he doing here? What does he want with me? Should I call Walker?* I take a few calming breaths and hold my hand over my stomach. *Please let me get through this with his father, and please Walker, come home.*

I re-joined the two men and offered coffee, but they declined, and I was told to sit. Mr. Reed's lawyer fumbled through his brief-case, while Mr. Reed regarded me in his usual cool manner. I prayed that I wouldn't get sick, or maybe that would have be a good thing for me to do. I didn't, and fearfully waited until he spoke.

"Ms. Mitchell, I have given you every opportunity to end your relationship with my son, but you defy my requests at every turn. You have left me with no choice but to strike at you in a way that you will understand." He turned to his lawyer and he handed me two sealed envelopes. I looked up at him, and Mr. Reed gestured for me to open it up. My hands were trembling with what I already knew what the envelope contained. I gasped and covered my mouth with the grainy images before me. It was the pictures of stills from the movie that was produced from my stolen pictures. I quickly ripped them up, threw them at his feet, and shot daggers with my eyes at Mr. Reed.

"What is this, Mr. Reed? You can't scare me with these pic-tures. As horrific as they are, I have told Walker about them, and he doesn't care. He knows this wasn't my fault, and I was completely victimized as well as the other girls that were involved."

"Ms. Mitchell, that may be true, but I don't think your future employers will be happy to know that they have hired a past porn star to teach at their institution, pretending to be a role model for young impressionable children."

"Mr. Reed, I am not a porn star! How dare you come in here and speak to me this way."

"How dare you defy me, Ms. Mitchell? Did you think that I was simply going to forget about that scene that *YOU* were responsible for on New Year's Day? You tried to turn my son against me, and that will not be tolerated."

"You can't blame me for that, Mr. Reed. You have alienated your son all on your own, with your continued interference in his and my life. You are doing it right now by threatening me once again. You need to leave."

"No, my dear, you are the one that is leaving. I will make sure those pictures get stapled to every single job application you apply for, so no parent will want you teaching their children. Aren't you curious what's in the other envelope? Please look inside." I tore open the envelope and found the deed to my grandparents' home, land, and business. I sank to my knees, and began to cry. I looked around and focused on the door, willing it to open with Walker walking through it.

"Why are you doing this to me? Please, Mr. Reed, why?"

He bent over to lift my chin, and he answered coldly. "You are the one that is doing this, Ms. Mitchell. Only you can stop it. As you can see, Ms. Mitchell, I own everything, and with one phone call, I can have everything your grandparents hold dear...leveled. And the life they have at this very moment will cease to exist." He looked at his watch, and I could almost hear the ticking of his Rolex. His lawyer held his head down almost in shame. "Like I said, Ms. Mitchell, all this can disappear if *YOU* disappear, and never bother my son again."

"Mr. Reed, please don't do this. I love your son, we are getting married, and I'm pre..."

"Pregnant? Yes, I am well aware, my dear. You and your bastard child will vacate my son's life today, and you are never to contact him again. It didn't have to be this way, Ms. Mitchell. All you had to do was end things with my son, let him be happy with Elizabeth. But no, you trap him by getting yourself pregnant. Well I don't care what you do, but Walker is out of your life. If you don't do exactly what I say, then you only have yourself to blame. What's it going to be, Ms. Mitchell? You can quietly leave here now, and leave your grandparents' lives intact, or I place my phone call?"

I can't take anymore. I managed to stand up and simply agreed to his terms. He had broken me and shattered my life to pieces. He won, and I had no choice. I couldn't let him hurt my family because they have sacrificed everything for me. I would not let his one phone call destroy their life. His lawyer handed me another envelope that contained a check for one hundred thousand dollars. I am to take this and start over. *I can't believe this is happening, and how the hell am I going to explain this to Walker?*

"Mr. Reed, I'm begging you, please don't do this. I love him so much, and he's never going to believe that I just left him. We have shared so much together, I can't hurt him like this. Walker will never understand me suddenly leaving him. We have made promises to one another, and today he planned on asking me to marry him. I have already said yes to him over and over again. This will completely destroy your son, Mr. Reed. Please I am begging you, don't make me leave him."

"I will take care of my son, Ms. Mitchell. You don't have to worry about him anymore. You have an hour to leave New York, and I don't expect to ever lay eyes on you again."

The two men stood and turned away from me. I was crying, shaking, as my world crumbled around me. This man completely decimated me in minutes. The devil himself appeared before me in the form of Walker's father. I had no choice but to obey him, or he would hurt my family.

I so wanted to stay and wait for my beloved to return, but Mr. Reed probably had people watching me. Now I know for certain that I was followed the other day. *How could he know that I was pregnant? I had just found out myself.* This man respected no one, especially me. I was carrying his grandchild, and he didn't care. He called our baby a bastard. He was the bastard. I looked to the door, still no Walker. I had no choice but to leave.

I collected what I had at Walker's apartment, and left him a letter with my tears that have fallen down on it. *He is going to be completely devastated when he returns home to find me gone. How can I do this to him?* I once again fought against my own conscience. *Should I stay and tell him everything? And risk destroying my grandparents? Mr. Reed has vowed to level everything that they have. I can't allow that to happen, it will destroy them if I don't do what he wants.*

So much for me being strong and fighting the great Phillip

Reed. He has me exactly where he wants me. I'm in a no win situation and if I stay and wait for Walker, I may be able to stop his plans for today, but it will only be temporary. He is a powerful man and is not in the position he is by sheer luck. He probably has taken down mightier adversaries than a small town girl like me. Then again, I do threaten him because he knows his son loves me, and that is the one thing he has no control over. This is why he is going after my family. My grandparents are my Achilles heel, and I would never let anyone willingly hurt them.

As I looked around the room, and remembered every bit of Walker, I begged internally for him to forgive me. I took our picture that he kept on his nightstand of us. It was a collage of four pictures of our happy times together. He said he kept the same one in his wallet and one at his office in his father's building. I never had the chance to get my own copy, so I stowed this one in my bag. As I entered the car that would drive me away from Walker's home and away from the only man that I would ever love, I already mourned his loss.

Silently, my tears constantly flowed down my cheeks. I held my hand to my stomach, the one connection that I had left to Walker. *I don't know how I'm going to fix this, but there has to be a way to stop this man. I can't let this be the end for Walker and me? We promised on our love that we would have our "Forever" I can't let this be it for us.*

I clutched my beautiful locket, and silently prayed on it. Walker told me this was his heart, and I belonged to him. *I will not be the one to break his. I will find a way back to you my love. I promise I will.*

THE END…FOR NOW
FOR REESE'S STORY.
WE CONTINUE ON WITH WALKER.

PROLOGUE

Phillip Reed

Sins of the father...

"SIR, FORGIVE ME for speaking out of turn, but you can still make this right."

"How, Miles? Tell me how I can turn back the clock, and undo what I just did to that poor girl? A girl who begged me on her hands and knees to accept her and allow her to be happy with my son... my only son. It's too late for me now, and too late for her. Did you make the call yet?"

"Our man at the airport should be checking in at any moment."

"I can't return to the office until I know for sure that she boarded her flight. Please call him now; surely the plane has taken off." My lawyer was about to call for a status when his phone began to buzz in his pocket.

"Jacobson." He answered curtly. He listened attentively to his call and then looked over to me. I watched and listened as Miles continued to relay my instructions to the caller.

"Listen to me carefully: do not leave the airport until her plane is in the air. Do I make myself clear?" He ended his call and looked over to me.

"Well?" I ask.

"Ms. Mitchell's plane is on the runway and waiting to take-off."

"How much longer before it does?"

"It should only be a few minutes, and then Torrance will call me back. Can I fix you a drink while we wait?"

"No amount of alcohol is going to help right now, Miles. He's waiting on my call, and then phase two will begin. Is everything in place and ready to go?"

"Yes, sir. Once your partner is satisfied, then he will make the necessary transfer, and you can put this nightmare to rest."

"That's where you're wrong, Miles. The nightmare is just beginning... for Walker."

My lawyers' phone buzzed once again. "Jacobson. Has the flight taken off? Excellent. That will be all Torrance. You can now return to your post."

I looked over to Miles, whose facial expression confirmed what I already knew. I couldn't bear to hear the words; it would only solidify what I had committed here today. *I ruined two lives, one being my son, and the other, Reese Mitchell. The woman he loved and who had captured his heart. I am a selfish man, this I know. I now have to make the call that will seal my fate with my deal that I have made with the devil.*

"Phillip, I've been waiting for your call. Is it done?"

"Yes, she's gone."

"Define gone?"

"I've done everything you've asked me to do. The girl is gone, now let's finish this." I was clearly getting angry at this point, but my partner was not satisfied with my answers.

"Reed, why are you being so vague with me? I asked you to explain yourself and yet you haven't, why?"

"I am not trying to be invasive here. Per my instructions, she was delivered to J.F.K. Airport and taken to her gate. My man waited for her to board her plane, and he did not leave until the plane was up in the air... Satisfied?"

"Yes, I am. I will allocate the funds immediately, and the investigation will be closed and sealed forever. Just remember, Reed.

Your part in this is not concluded yet. You still have to get Walker to California. He needs to begin his future as your new CEO of Reed Global. And of course, he needs to marry my Elizabeth."

"All in due time, Henry."

"No, his time has run out. It ran out last fall when he walked in-to your home with that girl on his arm. I've waited long enough and so has my daughter. You know what to do, Reed."

I pressed the intercom to my driver up front.

"Ralston, take me back to Reed Global."

"Yes, sir."

"Miles." My lawyer looked up at me, waiting for me to speak.

"I'll take that drink now."

PART TWO

Walker

CHAPTER THIRTEEN

What you don't know won't hurt you...

I CAN'T BELIEVE I've been here for more than three hours already. This is not how I envisioned today to be. As soon as my father arrives, I can return to my angel who probably is up by now. I promised her breakfast, but now it's way past lunch. I'm sure she will forgive me once I get down on my knee and finally present her with her beautiful ring that is burning a hole in my pocket. I would have proposed weeks ago, but with all of our traveling we have both done, and then having to deal with the whole Milan clusterfuck of a trip.

I hated to be mistrustful of her, but her drunken ass of a best friend led me to believe that she may have cheated on me. I was out of my mind, and then of course, I lost my head and argued with her. Freddy later explained what truly happened and I was beside myself. I didn't know if I should board a plane and bring her home, or wait for her to return to me. My second choice turned out so much better, she was completely taken by surprise, and we made love for days after our happy reunion.

I'm happy I waited to propose. My girl is not going to see this coming. Yes, she knows I plan to ask her. However, what she didn't know is that Lila, her grandmother, gave me the ring that will now be Reese's. The morning we left Georgia, Lila asked me to take a walk with her through the meadow. The same meadow that Reese and I had just made love in the night before, under the moonlight. I tried to focus on what she was saying, but my mind kept drifting back to Reese. Then her grandmother took my hands and cradled them in hers. She said to me, "Walker, I know you are a good man and love my granddaughter. Take this ring, and when you're ready, please present it to her. Tell her the story behind it."

Lila had told me that the ring belonged to Reese's mother. It was given to her by Daniel, Reese's father, and Lila's only son. It was an heirloom piece from their homeland of Ireland. Daniel always knew that Susan, Reese's mother, was the love of his life. He wanted to give her a ring that signified their forever love. Susan and Daniel were separated the summer before they began their senior year of high school. That was the summer that Daniel traveled with his parents to Ireland. His grandmother, who adored him, gave Daniel her ring for his love. This would be the last time Daniel would ever see his grandmother again, but he cherished the time they had spent together. She always wanted this ring passed down to her only grandchild. Daniel didn't know at the time, but accepting the ring would ultimately play a part in my future with his daughter, Reese.

I knew from the moment I saw her, somehow it would lead me to this moment. Not in a meadow with her grandmother, but the moment when I asked her to marry and be mine, forever. Lila hugged me and wished us well. I never had that type of closeness with my grandparents, or my parents for that matter, but I welcomed it with Lila and Thomas Mitchell.

I opened up the tattered box, and it sparkled back at me. This ring is breathtaking, and it holds so many memories behind it. I wonder if Reese will even remember it. She lost her mom at such a young age, and who knows if she wore her engagement ring the entire time she was married to Reese's father? No matter, this ring belongs to Reese, and with Lila's blessing, I had some minor improvements added to her ring. I'm lost in my thoughts, when Ralston walks in to greet me.

"Mr. Reed, your father has just phoned, and will arrive here shortly."

"Well thank you, but I need to be leaving. I located the missing files that caused the chaotic morning the IT team had, so now if you don't mind, I have somewhere I need to be." I go to leave, and this giant blocks my path to the door. "Ralston, what the hell? Step aside or I will go through you." *Yeah… fat chance of that happening, but it sounded good in my head. This guy is built like a building.*

"Mr. Reed, have a seat, and wait for your father to return please." He enunciated every word very slowly, telling me that I had no choice, but to wait.

I took my seat, as he also sat down. I decided I would use this time to try and get some information from him. "Ralston, I need something cleared up for me."

"Yes sir, what might that be?"

"Why were you to pick my girlfriend up at school, and bring her to meet with my father?"

"I'm sorry, sir, but I'm not at liberty to say."

"Well, I'm giving you permission to speak like the dog that you are, and tell me what I need to know."

"I was simply following orders. I do not know why she was requested. I was only to deliver her to Mr. Reed."

"She's not a fucking package, Ralston. She's a person who I happen to be in love with, and don't you ever go near her again. Do I make myself clear?" I stare down the giant before me and show no fear. He doesn't break eye contact with me, but simply answers my question.

"Yes sir, understood."

I practically knock my chair back when the door opens, and my father bristles in with Miles Jacobson, his lead lawyer, and friend.

"Hello, Walker, thank you for coming down here today. I hear we had a problem in the server room? I take it all has been resolved?"

"Yes, it has. Some files were not in their proper locations, and I managed to locate them and store them correctly. Everything is set for the transfer next week."

"Wonderful news. Now Walker, I need to discuss some other matters with you."

"Father, I have been here the entire morning and now most of the afternoon. Whatever you need will have to wait until tomorrow. My girl is waiting on me, and I need to get home to her."

"Walker, why don't you just phone her and explain that you have matters of business that require your attention. If you are to be CEO of my company, then surely you better get used to this."

"Father, let's not forget that it's *our* company, and I will be CEO of Reed Global. That's something *you* need to get used to. Have a nice day." The look on my father's face was priceless, but the bastard had it coming. Now home to Reese, where I belong.

CHAPTER FOURTEEN

Shattered...

I TRIED CALLING Reese on her cell phone, but kept getting her voice mail. I also tried calling my apartment, but again, no answer. I wasn't worried; she was probably in the shower or listening to music. Reese is a fan of Bach and Alessandro Marcello. For her Christmas present, I gave her the complete works of their music library to her. Reese nearly knocked me over when she discovered what the box contained. To me, it was just CD's, but to Reese, it meant everything.

I stopped to pick up flowers and dinner for us. I can't believe I had spent the entire day away from her. *Why hasn't she called me?* Even this surprises me, but I shrug it off. What I needed to take care of at the office could have waited, but, Dennis, our in-house genius was frantic and needed to be calmed. Arriving at my building, my doorman hurries over to me to collect my bags that I'm carrying. I wave him off and hurry to the elevator. As the doors close I see his head hung low avoiding eye contact. Strange? He usually is so welcoming with me, especially since my family owns this building. I shrug it off and tap my foot in anticipation. I can't wait to see my girl.

I enter my darkened apartment, and feel a sudden chill in the air. Geez, Reese! I would have thought the fireplace would have been on. I flick on the entry way lights, and see no others on. I call out to her. "Reese, baby where are you?" No answer back. I place her flowers and dinner on the table and search for my girl. I look in all the rooms on the first floor, no sign of her. *Calm down man, she's here somewhere.* I make my way up to the master bedroom taking two stairs at a time, calling out for her. "Reese, are you here?" I enter my bedroom and find the bed still a mess from our lovemaking the night before. She's not here. Where is she? My chest begins to hurt and I look to my armoire where Reese keeps her things, but it's completely baron. *What the fuck!*

Why would she empty the cabinet? I go to my walk-in closet next and find the same. Everything that belonged to Reese has been removed. I get this sinking feeling inside of me that something is terribly wrong, but what? I left her sleeping soundly, and if something was wrong, why didn't she call me? Okay Walker, calm the hell down. I will simply call her, and find out where she is. I sit on her side of the bed and reach for the phone, but my eyes find a letter instead. It was a sealed envelope with my name on it, and in Reese's handwriting. *Oh please God, please God, this can't be happening.* I just know my worst fears are about to come true. Trying to get my breathing under control, I take some deep breaths and pull myself together. This could be anything, calm the hell down, and man up.

My hands are shaking, but I manage to open the envelope and I see her beautiful handwriting, but my eyes also focus on the dried tear drops on my stationary. It reads...

My Dearest Walker,

This is the hardest letter I have ever had to write. I can't even begin to explain the reasons behind it, and I know you will never understand. I pray one day you will forgive me for the hurt I'm about to cause you. I'm sorry. I'm sorry I was a coward and didn't find the courage I needed to be honest with you last night. Instead, I led you to believe that we have a future together. I'm sorry, Walker, but we don't.

We are not suitable for each other, we never were. You have your new life waiting for you in California, one that will not include me. I have decided to pursue modeling full-time and will be leaving New York, today. With Freddy gone now, I have no reason to stay. I will never forget what we have shared and will keep you with me in my heart forever. I love you, Walker. Please forgive me for the choices I have made here today, it was my only choice. You need to move on without me, it is for the best.

Reese

Your only choice? What the hell! No reason to stay? I'm your reason, Reese! Why? This can't be real. This can't be happening. I fall to my knees clutching her letter to my chest, and now my tears are falling. No fucking way am I letting her just leave me and with only a note to say goodbye. This doesn't make sense at all, and I have to find her. I fold her letter into my pocket and immediately leave in search of her. I take the stairs not wanting to wait for the elevator and I almost collide with our doorman, Warren. He knows something, he has to. This is why he acted strange when I entered the building earlier.

"Warren, have you been here at your desk the entire day?" I ask him.

"Yes, sir, I have."

"Were you here when my girlfriend, Reese Mitchell, left?" He looks like he is about to throw up, he's hiding something. I can sense his body language. "Tell me right now, or your ass is fired."

"Sir, forgive me, I was here. Ms. Mitchell left hours ago. I helped her into a cab, and she drove off."

"What time exactly, I need you to remember."

"I'm sorry sir, but I don't. The lobby was quite busy today, and I was needed elsewhere."

"You just told me that you helped her, and now you say you were elsewhere. What aren't you telling me?"

"Sir, I only meant that I was busy with many tasks and I don't recall the time, but I did assist her."

I pinch the bridge of my nose. I am ready to lose my fucking mind. *Where is my woman?* I take a breath and look back to my very apprehensive doorman.

"I don't have time to sort this out right now, Warren, but I will be back. Something is not adding up and believe me, I will find out what it is." I turn away from him and run like my life depended on it. I'm so frantic that I leave my car behind, and run to Reese's apartment. I arrive to her place in Washington Square, where I see a small moving van. I enter her apartment to find it completely cleaned out. I call out for her again and again, but I am only answered by an older man who I recognize as Freddy's uncle.

"Young man, can I help you?"

"Mr. Mackelstein, do you remember me? My name is Walker

Reed. I'm a friend of your nephew, Freddy? And my girlfriend, Reese, shared this apartment with him."

"Yes, of course I remember. I'm sorry son, when you get to be my age, you tend to forget sometimes."

"It's quite alright. Can you please tell me where Reese is?"

"I haven't seen her, son. I stopped by to pick-up some mail for Freddy, when I found this." He handed me an envelope with keys in it and a note simply saying that she will not be returning to the apartment, and it can now be rented out. Her note sounded so final, as if she was not returning. None of this makes sense.

"Mr. Mackelstein, have you spoken to Freddy? Surely he must have known about Reese giving up the apartment."

"I'm sorry, Walker, but all I know is that Freddy is in Europe, and the last conversation I had with my nephew was very different than the one that is taking place right now."

"Which was what, sir? If you don't mind me asking." My heart was beating at a rapid pace, I felt lightheaded and needed to sit. Freddy's uncle must have sensed it, and offered me a bottle of water and a seat on the stoop. The apartment had no furniture left in it, not one picture on the wall, no sign of my girl. "Please, sir, what do you know?"

"I spoke to Freddy right before he left for Milan, and he told me that your girlfriend would be moving out soon and be joining you. Once that happened, I was free to rent out the apartment. I wasn't expecting to find this notice of departure. The apartment was cleaned and her belongings removed, so I called my guys to pick up the rest of Freddy's things. I'm so sorry, son, but that's all I know. I'm all finished here. Is there anything I can do for you before I leave?" Freddy's uncle asked me with concern in his voice.

"If you don't mind sir, can I have a few minutes alone here?"

"Of course, just please lock up on your way out." With my head in my hands, my world was falling apart around me. I picked myself up, and walked around the now empty rooms. I found myself in her bedroom. I can smell her perfume that lingers in the air. I breathe it trying to savor every bit of Reese.

"Where are you, baby? And why did you leave me?" Why did you run? My silent cries now turn to loud sobs and my knees buckle. I have no more strength, and I just fall to the floor. After what seems like forever I get up, my feet weak beneath me, and I feel like I can't breathe. I have to find her. I know exactly where to look.

I hail a cab and pay the driver an extra fifty to drive as fast as he can. I enter my building to find my father waiting for me... and speaking to Warren.

"Walker, there you are, son. Where have you been?" *Wrong time to fuck with me father. I feel the anger rising up within me as he stands there smugly.*

"Why in the hell is that your business? I have somewhere I need to be." I ignore my father's calls and hurry to the elevator, shutting him out. I pull down a bag from my closet, and throw in the first pieces of clothing my hands find. I need to get out of here and find Reese. I enter my living room to find my father and Ralston waiting on me.

"What in the hell are you doing in my apartment? And why is *he* with you?" I snarl at my father.

"Walker, your door was open. Ralston is my driver; it shouldn't be a mystery why he is with me."

"Father, I don't have time to play twenty questions with you." I look to Ralston who is blocking my way, again! "Step aside, or I will move you."

Ralston is enjoying this way too much at my expense. He speaks..."Walker, you're not going anywhere." *Oh hell no! Try and stop me.* That's exactly what the big ape does, he blocks me again, and this time I stumble back. Fuck this. I take a swing at him, almost breaking my hand, but it does catch him off guard. I almost make it to the door, until he hauls me back in.

"Get your fucking hands off of me!"

"Calm down, and I will." Shouts Ralston.

"Call off your dog, and let me go." I shout at my father, but he doesn't even blink. *What the hell is going on?*

"Son, please calm down and let me explain. I was simply stopping by on my way to meet your mother, and I find you in this state."

"Ralston."

"Yes sir?"

"Release my son."

He does exactly as he is instructed to do. Yup! The bastard is enjoying this way too much. Ralston retreats to a corner of the room, as I turn to speak with my father.

"That's just it, Father, why would you be just 'stopping by' when you knew I had plans with Reese tonight? I told you back at the office that I had somewhere to be, so why the visit?"

"Why the questions, Walker? You are out of control and behaving all paranoid."

"Like I said, I have somewhere I need to be, and I need to leave right now."

"Fine, go on, but when shall I expect you back? What shall I tell your mother?" I grabbed my bag as I exited my apartment. "Tell her I left to go find my heart." I stormed out to hail a cab and make my way to the airport.

I was able to catch the last flight to Georgia. I just arrived at the gate when the doors were about to close. I caught my breath and handed my first class ticket to the gate attendant. I finally began to calm down and ordered a drink. The flight attendant raised her eyebrow at me, but I gave her the "don't fuck with me look" and she served me my double scotch. I downed my drink and was offered another. I declined, and waved her off. I closed my eyes, and Reese took over my thoughts. Please God, let me find my girl. I need to hold her in my arms and help her. I don't believe her letter. All this time we have spent together has been real, something has driven her away, and god help the person that is responsible for this.

I take out her ring and get lost in it. I see myself sliding it on her finger and watching my beautiful girl light up with love for me. She is so happy, and her eyes are sparkling as much as the diamond that is now in its rightful place. Snapping the box shut, I vow to find Reese and bring her home. I am not letting her go without a fight. I snap my finger at the flight attendant and order another double.

CHAPTER FIFTEEN

Pottersville...

IT'S CLOSE TO midnight by the time I arrive and get settled in my hotel room. I want so much to go out to her grandparent's home, but it's too late for that. They are early risers from what I can remember. I will go see them first thing in the morning. I shower and try to get some sleep. Lack of food and too many drinks later, my head is spinning, and my stomach is churning. Room service brings me my very late dinner. I try to eat what I can. My body rejects the food, and my stomach does one final flip before I find myself empting the contents of my stomach into the toilet. I haven't gotten sick like this since my first year of college when I rushed during pledge week.

I crash down on my bed, while Reese takes over my dreams. My head is pounding. *Holy hell*! And what the hell is that sound? I look over to the phone that is ringing. I had forgotten that I asked the front desk clerk to give me a wake-up call. I quickly shower, and drive my rental out to Mitchell's Café. I enter the café, and the sweet smells of apple pie and cinnamon remind me of the last time I was here, and with Reese.

"Good morning, darling! What can I get you?" The friendly

clerk smiles up at me and wants my order.

"Good morning to you. May I speak to Lila or Thomas Mitchell? Are they here?"

"Sorry darling, the bosses usually don't come in this early. Can I get you some coffee?"

"Yes, please, and a scone to go." I drive out to their place, hoping to find Reese with them. As I pull up in front of their home, I don't see her grandfather's truck. *Please let them be home.* I knock on the front door and wait for an answer. No one comes to the front, so I walk to the back and repeat my knocking. No one is home, and I begin to make my way to my car when I hear the sweetest voice calling out to me.

"Walker dear, is that you, son?" I let out the breath that I was holding, and turn to see Lila, Reese's grandmother, standing before me. She's holding a basket of wild flowers. I don't know what comes over me, but the flood gates open and I almost crash into her arms. She drops the basket and holds me while I cry on her shoulder.

"Oh Walker, come in the house and I'll make you some tea." Here I am sniveling like a child, and she comforts me like a parent should. I can see why Reese loves her so much. I enter the familiar room that I visited only a few months ago. My eyes find hers. Pictures of Reese are all around the room, and I can't stop staring at the one of us sitting on Lila's mantle. This picture was taken on Thanksgiving. I want to just take it and hold it to my hurting heart. She gestures to me again to sit and talk with her.

"Walker, she's not here." Her grandmother sadly answers my unspoken question.

"Please, Lila, you have to tell me where she is. I found this letter yesterday at my apartment, it doesn't make any sense. I went to her apartment, and it's been completely emptied with no sign of Reese. I left her yesterday morning asleep in my bed, and came home to find her gone." I realize what I just revealed to her grandmother, because Lila was now blushing. I apologize for my slip, and she shrugs it off.

"Walker, if I knew where Reese was, I would be the first person to tell you. I'm so very sorry, but I really don't know where she is. She phoned me late yesterday afternoon and explained to me that she needed some time away. She said she would be leaving New York. I of course questioned her about it, but she only said not to worry about her and she would be in touch with me soon. Of course, I was upset, but I couldn't even tell her grandfather. He is away on a fishing trip with friends. I was beside myself with worry, but she also told me something else."

'Which was? Please, Lila, you have to tell me everything."

"She asked me to tell you that when you come looking for her, please let your search end here."

"What? Why on earth would Reese say that to you? Please, Lila, what have I done to push her away from me? I am dying inside without her."

"Oh Walker, I wish I knew. Someone put a world of hurtin' on my granddaughter, but it wasn't you. My girl loves you with all of her heart. She tells me so in every phone conversation we have. When she called, I begged her to tell me what's wrong. All she said was for me not to worry and that she would fix this. Walker, I don't know what 'this' is, but she's running from something, I can feel it in my bones."

Reese's grandmother took me in her arms and held me as I cried again. Here I was, a man, and again I was crying like a child. My heart was broken, and my love was gone. I could still feel her ring pressing against me in my pocket. I broke free of her hug, and I took it out. She covered her mouth in surprise when I handed it back to her. "No, Walker. This ring belongs to you now, and this is the ring that you will marry my granddaughter with."

"Lila, please don't make this harder for me. Reese is gone, and I have no idea where she is. I feel like she has sliced me wide open, and bled me dry. It wouldn't be right keeping the ring."

"Walker, for the last time, this is your ring now and you will keep it. My granddaughter will come back to you when she is ready to. I don't know what made her run or who for that matter, but the truth has a way of rearing its ugly head. You wait and see." Her words were just as painful as Reese leaving me. *Has someone made her leave me? Who could have done such a thing? Then as if the light just went off in my head, only one person comes to mind: my father...Phillip Reed.*

"Lila, forgive me, but I need to get back to New York. If you hear from Reese, can you please call me immediately? I love her so much, and I need to see her."

"I promise. Walker, please don't give up on her." *Give up on her? Like she gave up on me, and us?* I shove the ring back into my pocket. I hug Lila one more time and then head to the airport. I was so sure that I would find Reese today with her grandparents that I checked out of my hotel. I need to get back to New York as soon as possible, so I can confront my father.

The last forty eight hours are a blur to me. My body is exhausted from traveling and calling everyone I know to try and find some information. I even check with her professors at school. All they can tell me is that they were informed by administration that Reese had taken an academic leave from NYU. No one knows of Reese's whereabouts. My father is conveniently out of town when I arrive back in the city. My building's doorman, Warren, has been replaced by a new employee. His name is Randolph. I ask why he was replaced, and I'm told by the building manager that Warren retired. *Huh...another coincidence or just my father covering his long track of deception?* My apartment is still cold and empty without Reese. I'm so lost without her. No phone calls, no text messages, nothing from Reese.

My body is craving her touch. I'm remembering our last time together right here on this bed. She was spread out for me and waiting for me to make love to her. Our bodies were in sync with each other, we never missed a beat. Her breasts were made for my hands to hold, and her lips were made for me to kiss and suck on. I'm inhaling her scent that still lingers on her side of the bed. I'm the one that stayed. I'm the one that is tortured and broken. *Where are you baby? Please come back to me.* I plead with God, as if I am waiting for divine intervention to help me.

I need to speak with my father. It only took some flirting with my father's assistant to get the information I needed on his location. The company plane would be arriving at J.F.K. Airport around eight o'clock this evening and then he was off to the Midtown Club to meet my mother. I certainly don't wish to have another scene played out in front of her. I will just be waiting for him when he walks off the tarmac. One way or another, he will answer my questions and tell me what he did to Reese.

CHAPTER SIXTEEN

Confessions...

HIS PLANE IS on time. I stand in the shadows without Ralston seeing me. I watch my father walk down the stairs, as he glances around. What is he looking for? He looks guarded, as he should be. He's been avoiding me for days and he has to know his time is up. Just as the limo is about to leave, I open the door and slide in next to my father. He is not surprised, but Ralston hits the breaks. My father starts to put up the sound proof divider and instructs him to travel on.

"Walker, I've been expecting you. Why all the cloak and dagger? You didn't have to take the limo as if you were seizing it. You look like hell by the way. When was the last time you slept or showered?"

"Well, father, here's the thing. Reese… you remember her don't you? Well, she's missing, and I don't know where she is. So, yes, I not only look like hell, but I'm in hell without her. I want her back. Where is she?"

"What makes you think that I know?" He scoffs.

"I know you know. You have tried from day one to extricate her from my life and now you've succeeded. I will only ask you one more time, where is she?"

"Walker, I don't know where your Reese Mitchell is. Yes, it's true I never liked the girl. As your father, I want more for you, and she was not your match. Now Elizabeth is the one you should be focusing your attention on. I just saw her while in California. She asked about you."

Clenching my fists at my side, it will be a miracle if I am able to hold on to my control without hitting the smug bastard. I take one calming breath and look directly in my father's eyes. "You are either the most deluded motherfucker who ever walked the face of the earth, or you just play dumb really well. Who do you think you are talking to? I'm your son, you bastard. I know you and I know what you are capable of. You are not innocent in this; I feel it and would bet my life on it."

"Walker, if you ever speak to me in that manner again, I don't care what you believe your rightful place is in our company, I will cut your balls off, and serve them to you on the silver platter that you have been accustomed to your entire privileged life. I'm your father and you may not like me half the time, but you damn well will respect me. Do you understand me?" He issues his warning as his jaw clenches down.

"I will respect you, when you respect me. My life is my own and you will not control me! Today, tomorrow, or any day for that matter. You do not get to decide who I marry and who I choose to spend and share my life with. I'm done playing this game with you. I can't prove it now, but I will. I know you had something to do with Reese leaving me. When I do find her and confirm what I already know, you will not be able to hide from me. Fuck you and your empire." The car comes to a stop at a red light. I jump out from my father's car and never look back as I hear him call out to me.

"Shall I go after him, Sir?"

"No, Ralston, let him go. Please take me to the office."

As we drive through the city, I am haunted by Walker's words. His declaration of independence and truth gives me chills. As it is written in the bylaws of the company, and my father's will, once Walker graduates, all that is mine will now be his. In three short months, he can force me out and all that I've done would have been for nothing. He is brilliant, and I know with the right guidance and discipline, he can be spectacular. He just needs to get his personal life under control, and Elizabeth is the key. She has always had a way of leveling him out and making him see reason.

I am in an impossible situation. If I reveal my duplicity in Reese's leaving, then I risk losing my son forever. Olivia will divorce me, and I will quite possibly go to prison for the rest of my life. Townsend made sure to bury my crimes, and now I have to deliver my son to his daughter as payment.

I phone my wife from the office and regrettably cancel our dinner plans. I love my wife dearly and hate to disappoint her, but she is well accustomed to how I work. I just want the very best for my son, but it's the way that I've gone about it that occupies my thoughts at night. These are my sins...the ones that I will undoubtedly take to my grave.

Sitting behind my desk at Reed Global, I struggle to find solace in the quiet that is surrounding me. Walker calls this office the Throne Room. He may be right, with the relics that hang on the walls and the pristine pieces that fill this office. As I drink my finest scotch, my thoughts are interrupted by Miles, who is standing in my doorway.

"Sir, may I come in?"

"Miles, why are you in the office at this late hour?" I glance down at my watch. The dial is hard to read on account of my brain flooding with the scotch that I have now consumed since Walker ran from me.

"I took a chance that you might be here and wanted to give you an update on Ms. Mitchell."

"Yes, what about her?" I pour myself another drink while I wait to hear his report.

"She's in California, with her agent, Marsha Malin. She's renting a furnished loft, while she works out on the west coast." I let out a sigh and run my fingers through my hair.

"Miles, where in California?"

"She's modeling in Los Angeles, but she has a place outside of the city near the beach."

"What else do we know?"

"From what we know in our monitoring reports, Torrance has her routine down. She runs every morning up and down the beach. She reports to Elite's downtown office in Los Angeles, and only has been photographed with her agent or agency staff members."

"What about the baby?"

"As far as we know she's still pregnant, and hasn't seen a doctor yet. Torrance has only tracked her from her home to the office. When she finishes up for the day, she goes back to her loft."

"What am I doing, Miles?"

"Sir?"

"That precious girl is carrying my grandchild, and I forced her to leave my son and her entire life, because I am everything my son says that I am." I knock back my drink and lay my head down in my hands.

"Are you reconsidering the plan, sir? I just received confirmation this morning that all funds have been received and the company is back on track. Files have been sealed and the investigation to the building collapse has been closed. The few families of the workers that were killed have been amply compensated. If you go back on your word now, Townsend will make sure you go to prison."

"I'm well aware of what Henry Townsend is capable of. He's been my friend for twenty five years. He can be your best friend or your worst enemy, and right now I don't even know where I fit. Walker is completely destroyed by my manipulations and he is going to down spiral quickly if he doesn't find her soon. I know my son; he will not rest until he finds her."

My lawyer peruses the file he is holding and gives me yet another status. "He's already been to Georgia, sir."

"Of course he has, we knew that would be his first stop. I was sure she would have gone to her grandparents, but with Ms. Mitchell believing our threats, she was probably too frightened to risk it. I want you to keep tracking him, but use someone that Walker does not know. Keep him in the shadows, and I want to receive daily reports on his coming and goings. He is to return back to campus Monday morning, make sure he gets there. He just needs to complete his last course, and then he will be cleared for graduation. Once school is finished for him and we move him out to California, he will forget about Ms. Mitchell and concentrate on his future."

"Phillip, may I speak freely?"

"You're asking me now? By all means...what's on your mind?" I am about to pour myself another drink, and the bottle is grabbed from my hands. "What the hell! Miles, if you value your job, you will give me back that bottle."

"If you value your liver, you will stop drinking your guilt away tonight." He calmly says. He knows I won't fire him. He places the bottle on the bar and turns to me with his palms now flat on my desk. "Phillip, you still have the power to stop this. We can find another way to fight Henry, and your son can be reunited with Ms. Mitchell."

"No Miles, I can't stop it. Any power I may have had has now been ceased by Henry. He will never let me go back on our agreement. I have destroyed my son. I have destroyed that innocent girl. I am everything my son believes me to be. What I have done solidifies my place in hell. I deserve nothing less."

I get up from behind my desk, and stride over to my bar to pour another drink. I raise my glass to Miles. He is looking at me with disappointed eyes. I'm not surprised... another person I have failed. Yes he's my lawyer, but he's been my friend longer.

"To redemption and the sins I have committed. May God have mercy on my soulless soul." Slamming my glass down on the bar, I turn away from Miles and leave him standing in my office.

CHAPTER SEVENTEEN

Drowning without her...

WEEKS HAVE GONE by, and no word from Reese. I've called her grandmother every day since I left Georgia. Lila hasn't heard from Reese either. If she has, she's not telling me. I'm completely lost without her. I've called everyone we know, and our friends are also confused by her actions. The one person that I thought I could trust and could rely on to help me was Freddy, but he hasn't returned my phone calls.

I'm desperate at this point. I've hired my own private investigator to locate Reese. So far, still no leads to go on. I've questioned my father repeatedly and his answers are always the same. He emphatically denies having anything to do with Reese leaving me. As much as I love Reese and want her back, I still manage to make my classes. I've worked too hard to throw away my college career, but it's the nights that are the most difficult to face alone. I no longer feel her presence in my apartment or smell her perfume. I ransacked my home in search of a photo that went missing from my bedroom, my only conclusion was that Reese had taken it when she left… a parting gift from our relationship?

My mother has implored me to re-join the land of the living and put Reese behind me. How can I do that? I have no closure to our relationship. I left to go to work, and when I returned, I found her gone. None of this makes any sense to me, and I don't see how I will ever be able to move on from Reese. Until she faces me and tells me directly that we are over, I'm *not* moving on. Not that I would ever accept that anyway. She knows how much I love her and would lay my life down for her. I gave her that heart locket as a sign of our love and commitment for each other. How could she just lie to me like this? No! She wouldn't do that. I know she wouldn't. Someone scared her off, and I only can think to keep directing the blame toward my father. It has to be him, but again, why? What does he have to gain by making Reese leave? This is what I need to find out.

My week was short with spring break upon us. I had just left a meeting with my advisor, and he informed me that I had successfully passed my last course, and as far as my college days go, I was finished. He asked me if I would walk with the rest of my graduating class, and I told him that I would think about it. I'm quite sure nothing would please my mother more, then to see me walk with my class. Of course it would hit the New York papers and society page. How silly of me to want to miss a photo op for the Reed Family.

My parents planned on hosting a party in my honor up at their Hampton Estate. My mother begged me to say yes. and after listening to my mother drone on about it, I finally did concede. As long as the bar was fully stocked, I would attend my party and numb my pain while I endured it.

Just as I was about to leave for the Hamptons, the private detective that I hired appeared at my door. I was taken by surprise, but was hopeful that he located Reese.

"Mr. Reed, I hope I'm not catching you at a bad time."

"Of course not, John, please come in. Can I offer you a drink?"

"No sir, I'll be brief. I took a chance by stopping by here tonight. I know you've been anxious to hear news about your girlfriend." *It's all I want. I want Reese back.*

"So what's in the file? Spit it out, man!"

"I'm sorry sir, but not much. I've tracked her to California, Los Angeles to be precise. She is doing some modeling work out there."

"Are you kidding me? Los Angeles? This is good news. Have you talked to her? Let her know that I'm looking for her?"

"That's just it, sir. She was in Los Angeles, but not anymore. My men lost track of her three days ago."

"What the fuck? You knew where she was three days ago, and I'm just finding out now? What kind of game are you playing, John? Did you really locate her, or are you trying to derail me from finding her?"

"Sir, I work for you and you alone. I had other cases that needed my attention. I assigned my best men to Ms. Mitchell, and I had no reason not to distrust them or doubt their ability to track her."

"Then why did they lose her? Something does not add up, John. From the beginning of Reese leaving me, and New York, nothing about this sounds right."

"Sir, some people just don't want to be found. Here is my report and some surveillance photos from the last time my men spotted her."

"Let me see the photos." I take the envelope from John's hands and tear it open. I peruse each one, and my eyes immediately find something terribly wrong with the pictures that John has provided. The woman in these photos are not Reese. I would know my girl-friend anywhere, this woman is not Reese. "What the fuck? This is not Reese!"

I lunge at John, grabbing him by his neck. I grit my teeth as I demand to know what the hell is going on. He denies any wrongdo-ing, and he sticks to his truth. "Who put you up to this? Was it my father, Phillip Reed? Tell me now!"

John gets out from under me, and delivers a right hook to my jaw. I bounce back up and charge him with all that I have. He goes down crashing over my table and shatters the glass along with it. I'm now grabbed by two other men who I don't know. One holds my arms behind my back, while the other punches me in my stomach. John stumbles up, and calls them off of me. Too late, the damage is done. I could feel a rib, maybe two, broken, and blood is dripping from my brow.

"Get the hell off of me!" I shout at the men. They release me as John gives them a warning look.

"Both of you get out!" John shouts back. They leave my apartment, and I slump down to the floor.

"Mr. Reed, I'm sorry about that unfortunate incident. I did the job that I was hired for. I'm sorry I wasn't able to give you the answers you needed."

"Just get out, you lying bastard." He drops the files at my feet before walking out the door, never saying another word to me. I feel my ribs throb as I try to stand, but to no avail, I'm rooted to the floor. As I sink lower in my despair and feeling the broken glass under me, I silently whisper…this is rock bottom.

AS I CONTINUE to build on the lies I have created, I silently sit in the shadows watching the tall figure enter my car. With my drink in hand, I don't look over to him and just ask my question.

"Did you deliver the report and pictures, per my request?"

"I did, sir, but he didn't believe the woman in the photo was Ms. Mitchell. Mr. Reed became violent with me, and had to be subdued."

"Is my son hurt?" I feel as if I am choking on my words.

"He might have a few broken ribs, but I can't be sure. I was still trying to get my bearings after he struck me. My men not knowing the situation took down your son and subdued him. Mr. Reed, please know we never meant to do that."

I don't respond to his feeble excuses. "Here is your payment. This conversation never took place. Get out!" He simply takes the envelope from my hand and retreats in to the darkened night.

This was not how I wanted this to go, but it needed to happen to deter Walker from his futile attempts on locating Ms. Mitchell.

Enough time has gone by, and still he has received no word from her. So far, she has kept her end of the bargain, and stayed away. I call the one person that I know can get through to him, and make him see that Ms. Mitchell leaving him was for the best. It's time to put the next part of my plan in motion.

I scroll down my contact list and call the very person that can help me…help my son. She answers on the second ring.

"Elizabeth, Phillip Reed here."

"Hi, Mr. Reed, how are you?"

"I'm fine, dear… just fine. I'm happy to have caught you. Are you planning on attending our party for Walker this weekend?" She sighs on the line.

"Mr. Reed, I don't think that's a very good idea that I show up at your home. I have tried for weeks now to reach out to him, and he evades me at every turn. I don't know how to help him."

"Elizabeth, my son is very stubborn and he's nursing a broken heart right now, but you are the one person that can heal him. He cares for you very deeply, and I know you return his affections. Please don't give up on my son, and try again? It would make his mother and me so happy."

"I'll try, Mr. Reed, but I'm not sure what I can do."

"Please, Elizabeth, call me Phillip. We have known each other for far too long for these pleasantries. I just phoned the doorman at Walker's building, he hasn't left the city yet. Why don't you go check in on him and maybe you two could drive out together? Elizabeth, are you still there?"

"Yes, sir, I am. Okay, I will try stopping by, but I make no promises."

"That's all I ask, my dear. Good luck with my son, and I will see you both tomorrow."

I let out the breath that I was holding while speaking to Elizabeth. Randolph has informed me that he hears sounds coming from my son's apartment. Thank god he's not badly injured. Elizabeth will find him, help him, and then I can finally report some good news back to her father to get him off my back. She has to get through to him, she just has to. I wait for more than an hour observing my son's building, and then I see Elizabeth step out of a cab and enter inside. I breathe a sigh of relief and signal my driver to take me home.

CHAPTER EIGHTEEN

Elizabeth

I love you my friend. Please let me help you...

ENDING MY STRANGE call from Phillip Reed, I struggle with my internal indecisiveness. Walker is in need of help. He has shut out the world after his girlfriend suddenly left him. I question why? They were clearly in love, and he repeatedly told me how he felt about her. After his very public display of affection for her, I knew I had lost any chance of ever being with Walker. Was his father right? Am I his match? No matter what, I will always be his friend first. He needs a friend who he can trust. He will hate it, but I will be that friend.

I arrive at Walker's building and casually step inside. His very nervous doorman walks quickly behind me as I reach the elevators. I think to myself. *Don't worry sir, I won't have you fired for not doing your job.* I turn to greet him.

"FORGIVE ME MISS, but it's customary to announce guests." Not knowing this man personally, I look over to his shiny name badge that graces his well pressed jacket.

"I understand that...Randolph, but Mr. Reed is a very close friend of mine, and I'm sure he will see me."

Not questioning me, he steps aside.

"Very well miss, I'll escort you up."

I raise my hand up and halt him where he stands. "No need to do that, I know the way, but thank you."

As I wait for the elevator to arrive on his floor, I silently pray that I can help my friend. I love him so much and all I want for him is to be happy. I go to ring his bell and see the door slightly opened. I reach into my purse for my can of Mace and go in with guarded steps. I call out to Walker and hear no response until I see him slumped down on the ground and covered in blood.

"Oh my god, Walker! What happened to you? Who did this to you? Were you robbed?" I hear the panic in my voice as I kneel down to help Walker. Oh how my heart hurts, as I take in my broken friend.

"REESE, YOU'VE COME back to me. Oh baby, I need you so much." He gazes into my eyes and grabs me by the nape of my neck toward him. Crashing his lips onto mine, he thrusts his tongue in my mouth, and although I know I'm not Reese, I welcome his kiss until he realizes who I am. He suddenly pulls back.

"Elizabeth? What are you doing? Why are you here in my apartment?"

Now I'm the one that is taken back. "I can ask you the same question. I came here to check on you, and I find you injured. And your door was opened, by the way. *You* kissed me, Walker. Are you drunk?"

"I'm sorry, Elizabeth, I don't know what came over me. I think I hit my head, I don't feel so well."

"You smell like a brewery, no wonder you feel like shit. Come on, let's get you cleaned up, and if you are really hurt, I'll take you to the emergency room."

"What would I do without you?" he asks me, as I easily get lost in his beautiful eyes.

I wrap his arm around my shoulder to help him off the floor. I softly answer his question. "Let's hope you never have to find out." *Please let me love you Walker, and make you forget about her.*

He's struggling against me. "Can you stand, Walker?"

"Yes, just give me a minute." I help him into his bathroom. I wash his face with a warm cloth to see where he's hurt. He has a small cut above his eye; I don't think it will need stitches. He lets me tend to him. It feels so good to help him, and he's allowing me to. He winces in pain when I touch his stomach. I slowly lift the hem of his t-shirt and pull it up and over his head. I'm treated to the sight of his beautiful chest and ab muscles. He is perfectly defined, but I do notice some bruising on his side.

"What happened here?" I point to his ribs.

He scoffs. "A…disagreement."

"That's all I get? Come on, Walker, what happened here to-night?"

"It's not your problem, Elizabeth. Please just let it go."

"Okay, I will for now. Can I take a look at your ribs?" He nods, and I carefully examine him. I don't even know if Walker knows this about me, but I am a trained E.M.T. While I was still discovering myself back in my freshman year of college, I decided to get certi-fied in this area. It drove my parents crazy, but it was something to do. Turns out, I was pretty good at it. I of course didn't pursue this as a profession, but I never forgot what I learned. After examining Walker, I concluded that his ribs are most likely bruised. He's not having any difficulty with his breathing. As a precaution, I wrapped his ribs with a tight bandage and secured it with some pins. He didn't want to go to the hospital, so this would have to do.

"Okay my patient, you're good as new." I try to smile to lighten his darkened mood.

"Am I, Elizabeth? I don't think I will ever be the same again."

"You will, Walker, you just have to give it time. Do you want to talk about it? Maybe I can help?"

"The only one that can help me is Reese, and she's gone. I want to die Elizabeth, just fucking die, and finally be free of this night-mare that I'm living with."

Slap! Elizabeth shakes her hand.

"What the fuck, Elizabeth! Why in the hell did you hit me?"

"I hit you because you said something so stupid. How could you, Walker? So your girlfriend left you, oh poor you. You think you're the first guy to ever have this happen to him? Pull yourself together, and grow the fuck up!"

The room is beginning to spin, and I lash out at my only friend. Here she is trying to help me and all I feel right now is hate. I scream at the top of my lungs. "What do you know about it anyway? Tell me, Elizabeth! What do you know?" I find myself grabbing my friend by her delicate arms, and begin to shake her.

She never did take my shit. "Get your hands off of me! What the hell is wrong with you?"

All my fight is gone. I simply give up. "Go home Elizabeth, there is nothing for you here."

"I'm not going anywhere. You need me Walker, please don't shut me out, or turn me away."

"I need Reese. She is all that I need."

"Well Walker, she's not here. I'm here and I need you. Can't you see how much I love you? I've always been here for you. You've never seen what's right in front of you, someone who loves you and will devote herself to you, if you let her. I'm right here, Walker! Please see me?"

"Elizabeth, you don't know what you're saying. You deserve so much better than half of a man that wants someone else. You are my best friend, and I can't hurt you like that. Please just turn around and GO now. Get out!"

"No! I'm not going anywhere." She is determined to drive me over the edge with her stubbornness. Her beauty doesn't escape me. I'm not blind. Elizabeth Townsend is beautiful, intelligent, and simp-ly kind hearted. She is like no other in our circle of friends. Yes, at first she was cool to Reese, but I know it comes from a good place. I know she loves me, but always stepped aside anytime someone new came into my life. Now she stands before me, and I can take her right now, and she would be willing to submit to me without question. Can I do that to her? I'm not drunk enough.

"Come here." I instruct her. I was already feeling guilty for raising my voice at the one person that has never let me down. I can't say the same for me. She once again is at my side and willing to do anything to comfort me, even offering her beautiful body. Elizabeth, with no fight left in her, walks easily into my welcoming arms. I fold her into me and whisper "Thank you" in her ear. I kiss the top of her head and hold her for a few minutes. Savoring her touch and welcoming the comfort of her embrace. I lift her chin, and find myself getting lost in her eyes. I see the love she feels for me. She deserves so much more.

"It's late, how about we order some dinner and you stay the night." Her eyes now light up, and I can almost see a sparkle. I have to be careful not to lead her on, so I rephrase. "You can have the guest bedroom, and I will be in my room." I don't miss the disappointment in her eyes, but she nods and goes to my kitchen for the menus. I haven't seen anyone so familiar with my home since Reese, but I remain quiet and leave Elizabeth to it, while I change my clothes.

I phone my mother, and I tell her that she can expect me tomorrow late morning. She bids me good night, and I find Elizabeth waiting for me by my fireplace.

"I hope you don't mind, it was a bit cool in here." Visions of making love to Reese flash through my memory.

"I don't mind." I lied. "Elizabeth, I need you to understand that I'm in love with Reese, and I am not giving up hope on finding and reconciling with her. I don't know why she left, but I fear I will never be able to move on until I know for sure. I meant what I said on New Year's. I care for you very deeply, but my heart belongs to Reese and I can't envision the thought of hurting you. Do you understand?"

"Walker, I'm no fool, but I can't help that my heart only wants you. I have loved you for as long as I can remember. Please don't give up on love and the possibilities that love can bring to your life. I know I can make you happy. Please think about it? Okay?"

"Okay, Elizabeth, I'll try." Her eyes light up like diamonds, while my heart continues to ache for the one that I love. I know just by agreeing to think about it, I have done the unthinkable, and have undoubtedly led her on. I told her what she wanted and needed to hear. Yes, I'm a bastard, but I can't help what my heart wants.

Dinner arrives shortly after our talk, and I honestly enjoy the food that Elizabeth has ordered for us. I can't remember the last time I really ate. I've lost some weight, and it's been way too long since I went a few rounds with my trainer. My ribs are killing me right now, so I don't think I could fully work out, but maybe a swim in the morning before the long drive out of the city.

I had taken something for my sore ribs and I was beginning to feel sleepy. But as much as I fought off Elizabeth's advances, I didn't want to be alone. She's the first woman that's been in my apartment since Reese, and she is just so familiar to me. God! I hate to even be fantasizing about Elizabeth, but she is too fucking beautiful. Her ass is perfectly round in her jeans. As she bends over, I can see her perfect shaped breasts protruding from her opened blouse. My dick is pressing against my jeans, and it's been so long since I've had sex. I can't do this to her, it's not right. I have to just excuse myself and take a cold shower.

I barely can find my voice when I call out to her that I'm going to bed. Elizabeth comes rushing over to me, and she wraps her arms around my neck and kisses my cheek. I try to pull away from her, but I no longer can resist her ruby lips on mine. She kisses me and now is holding my face in her hands, and for the first time I'm welcoming someone else's touch. *What the hell am I doing? No! I can't do this to her! No matter how my betraying body is responding to her?*

I pull away from Elizabeth. She stands there in shock, and I simply say good night, and leave her to watch me walk away from her. I enter my bedroom and slam the door behind me.

I crawl into bed, hold Reese's pillow, and try to breathe in any scent left behind.

"Please baby, come home to me." Darkness finally consumes me, and I fall into a deep sleep, dreaming of only Reese.

CHAPTER NINETEEN

The Party

SCRUBBING MY HANDS over my face, I lay here in my bed. Last night was not a dream. I got my ass kicked from two goons that I employed to help me find Reese. My ribs are fucking killing me, and I'm dreading the drive out to the Hamptons today.

As I make my way downstairs, I hear sounds coming from my kitchen. Knowing my housekeeper is not here can only mean that Elizabeth indeed stayed the night. I can see the happiness written all over Elizabeth's glowing face, as I enter my kitchen. This morning I am treated to the sweet smells of fresh rolls and coffee. For a brief minute, I had thought Reese had returned to me and surprised me with breakfast. *Get a grip, man!* It pains to me believe that she may be truly gone, but it's the love that I have for her that keeps me hopeful.

My appearance is much better from how my friend found me last night. I showered and dressed before greeting Elizabeth. I knew in my heart she was disappointed that we slept in separate bedrooms. After hearing her declaration of love for me, it was hard to not just take her where she was standing. My conscience won in the end, and

I knew I couldn't hurt her in that way.

I don't even know how she managed to prepare the breakfast she had waiting for me, but my table was set, and I had many choices to feast on. Hell, I didn't even know I had food in my fridge?

"Good morning, sleepy head. How did you sleep?" Her voice laced with concern.

"Fine, thank you for asking." Looking around the room, my apartment was sparkling clean, and Elizabeth was just smiling up at me. "How did you do all of this?" I gestured with my hand.

"I can't take all of the credit, but I did do most of it. Your housekeeper arrived a bit early for my taste, but got busy cleaning up last night's disaster. I quickly went home to change and grab my bag for the weekend. Along the way back over here, I stopped at the Italian bakery you like and picked up all of your favorites. The grocer is nearby as well, so I picked up what you didn't have in your refrigerator, which by the way was everything. I almost scolded your housekeeper for not stocking your kitchen, but in her defense, you never gave her the shopping lists like you normally do."

"Thank you. I really mean it, thank you."

Her eyes filled with tears. Shit! This is not what I want to see right now. It pained me beyond reason when Reese would cry. I can't take it. I do what seems natural, and I take Elizabeth in my arms and hold her. She returns her affections and we stand quietly in each other's arms. I lift her chin up with my finger and tell her, "No more tears today, I simply can't bear it." She gracefully wipes her eyes with a napkin, and we enjoy the meal she has prepared for us.

"How are the ribs? Are you still in pain?"

"They smart a bit, but I'll be fine."

We finish our breakfast in silence and make our way out of the city. Our drive to the Hamptons is a quiet one. I'm deep in thought about Reese, but also about facing my family. I don't want to hear, "I told you so" from my father. I still can't prove he had anything to do with Reese leaving me, but I'm exhausted, and I just need to clear my head. Elizabeth is more than willing to fill any void I require.

I look over to my friend who is leaning on my shoulder. "Elizabeth, wake up, we're here." Her eyelashes flutter, as she stirs in her sleep. She has been sleeping for more than an hour now, and so peacefully.

"Hey," she says as she stretches out her neck. "How long was I asleep?"

"About an hour or so. I think you needed it after our long night. Thank you again for taking care of me, friend."

"Walker, stop thanking me for something that comes natural for me. I want to take care of you, love you, and be so much more to you than a friend."

Another declaration! *Please make her stop, or I will lose all sense of my control, and fuck her right here in my car.*

I say nothing. The gates open, and I continue to drive up to the main house where my mother is waiting to greet me. She's not alone. Henry and Gail Townsend are also there and looking too happy for my taste. Seeing me arrive with their daughter will only flame their wants for me and Elizabeth to be a couple.

Her father opens her door, and takes her hand to help her out of my car. My mother is beaming at me and places two kisses on my cheek.

"I'm so happy to have you home, my son. It has been far too long since your last visit." My last visit was with Reese. *How could I forget? It was the first time you met her, and father immediately had taken a dislike to her. Yeah, good times.*

"If you'll excuse me, mother, I'll be upstairs in my room."

"You will do no such thing, Walker! This party is for you, and we want to celebrate our son today. Please say hello to the Townsend's, and try to enjoy yourself." My mother pleads with me, and then flashes her infamous, "You will do this for me" smile.

The house staff takes our bags, and I'm left standing there while Elizabeth and her parents make their way over to my mother. I feel trapped with no escape. Now I have her father approaching me.

"Hello Walker, so nice of you to bring our daughter here with you today. I never liked Elizabeth driving alone, especially with such a long drive. *It's like three hours, tops! Where is he going with this?*

"It was no trouble at all, sir." I shake his hand, and his wife gives me a quick hug. "How are you doing, Gail?" Her mother is truly one of the kindest women I have ever met. She's very down to earth. Although they have money, she lives her life in a simple way.

"I'm doing well, Walker. Thank you for asking. I just had a check-up last month, and happy to say that I am still cancer free." Elizabeth's mother had a scare a few years back with breast cancer, but her doctors caught it very early and she has been in perfect health since. Elizabeth didn't take the news well at the time, but I assured her that her mom would be fine. I was the first person she confided in when she found out. I was happy that I could help my friend. This is one of the reasons why I can't hurt her. She is too good of a person for me to just use to dull the pain from losing Reese. I need Elizabeth in my life as my friend, more than she knows. She is one of the few people that I can trust.

"That's great news, Gail. I hope your charity event brought in many donations for this worthy cause."

"Yes, it was a success. We raised over a million dollars for our charity. Your mother and Elizabeth worked their magic with our sponsors and contributed many hard working hours to the event planning."

I roll my eyes. "Well, don't give Olivia too much credit." I wink at my mother. "She loves this and probably could organize it in her sleep." Now that the pleasantries are said and done, I was exhausted and ready to break away to my room.

"Walker, a word please?" I sigh and take a walk with Henry Townsend. "Thank you again for driving my daughter out here with you. Like I said, her mother and I worry when she travels alone."

Is he serious? *She's a big girl who can take care of herself; I have no doubt about that. Cut the apron strings a bit, and let her breathe! She had no problem last night showing and telling me what she wants.*

"I was happy to do it, sir. Please excuse me, I'm tired and I want to be alone."

"Walker, that's just it. You're not alone son. You have an entire home filled with friends and family that want to celebrate you today. Can you please try to have a good time? Don't disappoint us today." *What the hell? Why is my personal happiness now important to Henry Townsend?*

"Excuse me, sir, but why are you so concerned about me? This party is no different than the hundreds of parties my mother has thrown over the years. I'm not in the mood to be put on display today, and I didn't fucking ask for this damn party to begin with."

"Walker, I would think twice about using that language in front of me again. All that I have asked of you is to try to have fun. What is the problem here?"

"Sir, I am no good to anyone right now, especially Elizabeth. I am drowning in my own pain right now. I don't care to spend time with anyone. The only comfort I'm seeking right now is the unopened bottle of vintage scotch that is up in my room." He looks disappointed in me after I proudly say that I would rather get drunk than be with his daughter.

"Just try, son. You have so much to look forward to. This party is a way of closing one door and opening another. You can walk through that door with my daughter, if you just open your eyes to what is in front of you." With that last piece of advice, he turns and walks away. I am in a state of play right now not knowing what move to make.

As I finally make my way up to my room, there he stands, Phillip Reed. My father of course is guarded with me, never knowing how I will react to him. The feeling is mutual, and I am so not having this conversation with him.

"Hello, Son." He extends his hand out to me, as if I was a business associate.

"Father," I reply curtly.

"My apologies for not being here upon your arrival, I had matters of business that required my immediate attention."

"No worries, I survived. Now, please excuse me."

"Can you spare a moment of your time for me?"

"Father…that is all I've been doing for the past hour. I'm tired, and I want to be alone!"

"Walker, please?"

I move past him, and gesture for him to come in and sit down. He all too eagerly moves past me, and sits on my sofa.

"I know you have been angry with me, but I assure you that your anger is misplaced. This is hard for me to say to you, but I am truly sorry for the state of affairs you are in right now. No parent wants to see their child hurting in the manner you are right now." *Who the hell is this man? And what has he done with my father?* I don't even have a response to this. He has never talked to me in this way before, and I am completely taken off guard here.

"I am who I am, Walker, I make no apologies for anything I do in this life. You are my son, and I will not pretend to want certain things for you. Your future happiness is everything to me and your mother. You know who I want you to choose as your partner, this is no secret. It would make your mother and me extremely proud if you marry Elizabeth." Holding my head to shut him out. *I can't do this today!* "Eventually you will move on from Ms. Mitchell and find happiness again."

I silently count to ten in my head. Here sits my father, who I can't decide is actually being genuine with me… or once again doing that thing where he shoves bullshit lies down my throat while calling it caviar. He hated Reese, and I still feel it deep down that he is not innocent with her leaving me. At this moment, I have no fight left in me, and I simply try to appease my father the best way I can.

"If it's all the same to you, father, please don't concern yourself with my personal life. We've been down this road before, and it never turns out good for either one of us. I don't need or care to hear one more time *who* is best suited for me to bed, marry, and have children with. I'm fucking done with the advice and the fake condolences for my broken heart. Now please show yourself out, and let me be. I will join the party when I'm good and ready to do so." I can't tell if my father is angry or proud of me with my act of rebellion, but he stands and leaves me alone in my room. I take out my bottle, and begin to drown very slowly in the abyss of my own personal hell... Reese.

Here we go again...

"WALKER, WAKE UP! You can't miss your own party." I jerk up suddenly, almost taking a swing at Elizabeth.

"What the hell, Elizabeth! What are you doing in here, get out!" I feel like I'm going to puke, and that's exactly what I do. Thank god Elizabeth saw it coming, and handed me the wastebasket. I emptied all the contents of what I had in my stomach, on top of all the alcohol I consumed. My body was racked with the dry heaves. I began to shake, and I vomited once more.

"You idiot, Walker! Oh god, I hope you don't have alcohol poisoning." I vomited one more time, and I think I was done. She wrapped up the bag and tied it off. I went into my bathroom to brush my teeth. I walk out to find Elizabeth with her hands crossed over her chest, with a look of sheer disappointment. I guess she should get in line; it seems I've been hurting everyone that tries to help me these days.

"Are you okay?' her voice is laced with sympathy. She never could stay angry with me for long.

"I'm fine, thank you again for helping me. Elizabeth, please go."

"I can't. I've been sent up here to escort you to your own congratulatory celebration. Here is your tux, get dressed, now!"

"Aren't you the bossy kitty cat? What if I don't want to get dressed, and join my party?" Now I'm just messing with her for the thrill of pissing her off. Elizabeth could hold her own with me, she always could.

She eyes me up and down, and then she does something completely out of character. Elizabeth takes her hair down, gives it a shake to make it look all wild and untamed, gliding her tongue over her top lip. *Fuck that was hot.* Images of Reese, flash before my eyes. She did almost the same act of sexiness the first time we made love.

"Have it your way, Walker. I guess I'll have to undress you myself." She grabs the hem of my t-shirt and begins to lift it over my head. I grab her hands and hold her in place. I can see the fire ignite in her eyes. She wants me, oh yeah. I think she would do just about anything for me at this moment. Why am I giving her the green light? Because I'm a guy who wants to get laid, and Elizabeth is right here and willing to give herself over to me and my desires... *Damn you Reese for fucking leaving me!*

"I can get dressed on my own." I say to her as I release her wrists.

"Are you sure? I don't mind being … of assistance."

"I'm positive. I'll be down in a half hour, I promise. You can go tell my keepers that they have my word." She smiles and kisses me on my lips.

"Save me a dance tonight, or two." Elizabeth sashays out of my room, and I'm left standing there with a throbbing dick.

I let the hot water cascade over me, and I silently pray for some kind of sign that I will make it through this night. I'm such a bastard for playing with Elizabeth's head and heart. She has been nothing but a good friend to me, and I'm an asshole at every turn with her. I don't want to be here, that much is clear. Just for tonight, I'm going to put my bullshit aside, and my hurting heart, and try to be the friend she knows me to be. Please god, don't let me fuck up again with her.

I check my cell phone before I make my grand entrance. My phone inbox is full of text messages from friends congratulating me on early graduation. I have several missed calls from a couple of weeks ago, to a few days ago. I don't recognize the number, and dial it back. The automated message tells me that the number has been disconnected. Strange? I don't delete it. I know of some hackers that may be able to trace it for me. It could be a lead on Reese?

No matter what my betraying body is doing with Elizabeth, my heart belongs to Reese and Reese only. *Wherever you are baby, please feel my love, and come back to me.* Tucking my phone in my pocket, I make my way down the grand staircase.

Elizabeth is waiting for me at the bottom. I tuck her arm into the crook of mine, and admire how beautiful she looks. She has now tamed her long locks, and tied it back.

"It's time, Walker. You are the master of the room. Are you ready?"

I cock my head to one side, and wink at her. "As I'll ever be.".

CHAPTER TWENTY

More than friends...

"DANCE WITH ME, Walker? I love this song." The look in her eyes was a look that was slowly breaking my resistance down. Her eyes are shimmering. For the first time, I can really see how she feels about me. Her eyes say it all, along with her body. I'm rooted to where I stand. I am craving touch again. She senses my fear, but gently takes my hand in hers and leads me to the dance floor. "Have you ever really loved a woman" is playing right now by Bryan Adams. I guess it's a fitting song, but honestly at this party I would have thought my mother would have hired a sixteen piece orchestra, not a DJ. She never ceases to surprise me.

Curious eyes are on us, as Elizabeth's hands travel up my back and find their place around my neck. I inhale the intoxicating perfume she is wearing and lose myself in the music. I feel light feather kisses behind my ear and slowly down my neck. I close my eyes and allow myself to enjoy it. I feel guilty for betraying Reese, but I'm not the one that left. I need this now…to feel alive again. The song ends, our bodies still connected. My body is telling me to kiss her right here, right now, but something stops me again. I pull away from her. I kiss her forehead and whisper, "Thank you for the dance." She looks dejected, crushing my already damaged heart into more crumbling pieces. As much as I physically want her, I won't hurt her like this. I take her hand to my lips and place a chaste kiss upon it. I can't bear to look at the disappointment in her eyes. I quickly turn away from Elizabeth and make my way over to the bar.

"What can I get you, sir?"

"I'll have a Chivas, make it a double, neat."

"Make that two," my father signals to the bartender. "Having a good time, Walker?"

"I don't know father, you tell me? Have I been social enough?"

"One dance with a lovely woman is not nearly enough, wouldn't you agree?"

"It made Elizabeth happy, I owed her that much. It's all I'm capable of right now." I swirl the amber liquid around in my glass before downing it in one gulp. I can feel the burn slowly make its way down my throat. I order another.

"You may want to slow down on those, son. Come, I have people you need to meet." I reluctantly follow my father, but not before downing my drink. I need liquid courage to get through this night.

A couple of hours later after rubbing shoulders with CEO's and various business associates of my father, I was beyond done, but my mother was not. She and my father took their place at the podium to say a speech in my honor. I looked around the room for Elizabeth, but she was nowhere to be seen. I guess I was on my own to endure it.

My mother called for everyone's attention, and then my father began to speak.

"On behalf of me and my lovely wife here, Olivia, we would like to extend our warm gratitude for all of you coming together and celebrating with us." *Applause*...I took in a deep breath and continued to listen to my father's speech.

"For those of you who do not know this already, my son here will be joining me in California as we take our company, Reed

Global, to the next level. There was a time when I considered taking Reed Global public, but I was well advised not to do that and keep it privately owned and operated by the Reed men. I am proud to say that I will be passing the reigns over to its rightful heir, my son, Walker Reed. He has made me one proud father today. He has graduated from New York University with honors, and leaving in hand degrees in Business and Economics. Although he is young, I truly believe he is ready to take Reed Global into the next century with his innovative thinking and creativity. Together, side by side, we are going to change the face of business. Stay tuned… *Applause!* Please raise your glasses, and let's hear it for the guest of honor, Walker Reed!"

I'm greeted with thunderous applause. One thing my father is good at is working the crowd to his advantage. He is, after all, the master of his universe.

To say the least, I was completely thrown by my father's well-prepared speech. Not one day my father, has he ever spoken to me with pride and admiration in his tone? I know this is for the crowd tonight, and for my mother. This is the path that I have chosen to take. I must now step up and join my father on the stage, and officially fill the shoes that are my legacy. I nod my head and begin to walk through the crowd, as I am patted on my shoulders and shake hand after hand. Lastly, before reaching the stage, I'm greeted by no other then Elizabeth.

"Congratulations, Walker. I'm so proud of you." She kisses me on my cheek and gracefully steps aside so I can make my way up the stairs. My mother embraces me, while my father shakes my hand. I move toward the microphone, and look out to the room. All eyes are on me, waiting with anticipation for what the new boss will say.

"THANK YOU FOR joining me and my family here in our home tonight. I'm not one for the spotlight, but thank you mother, you once again have outdone yourself. I have known many of you for my entire life, and to those who I have met tonight, I look forward to working with you, doing exactly what my father said...taking our company into the next century. I can promise you this. Reed Global will take on a new look with me at its helm. I believe in global energy, innovative thinking, and creativity. I, along with our design team, will also participate on projects that I hope to one day make my personal mark on. Not only did I graduate with Business and Economics degrees, but I also bring with me a degree in Architecture and Design. I am most proud of this, because it is where my heart lies, and it will help me be the CEO that Reed Global needs to take the next step into the future."

ELIZABETH IS LEADING the applause as I make my way down the stairs and into her waiting arms. "You are fabulous. Why didn't you tell me about the Architecture degree? I am so happy for you. Does this mean that I have a job on your design team?" She smiles and bats her long eyelashes at me.

"Send in a resume, and my assistant will get back to you." She laughs, and her sweet voice echoes through me like a song. Elizabeth is truly happy for me, and for the first time in a long time, I'm actually pretty happy myself, that is until my father makes his way over to me.

"Well, son, that was quite the speech. Let's get a drink, shall we?" I roll my eyes. He's pissed. What else is new?

Henry joins us, and he congratulates me. "How wonderful to hear your surprising news, son. You did well, and I for one look forward to working with you. Townsend Development is always looking to branch out and work with the next big thing... or shall I say my competition?"

I smirk at his invitation. I love a challenge...this is the one of the few things I have in common with Phillip. "Whatever works for you, Henry. I'm not worried. A toast to our companies and their future successes." We raise our glasses, and I down my drink. With the pleasantries out of the way, my father is glaring at me.

"Walker, a word please." We excuse ourselves, as my father leads me into his private study. He slams the door behind him. "Once again, thank you for embarrassing me in front of our guests. You could have warned me on what you were going to say. To hear you also received a degree that I wasn't aware of, completely derails me, Walker. Why do you continue to defy me at every turn?"

"First of all, father, it wasn't an act of defiance. I always loved the concept of designing my own building one day. You never listened to me when I wanted to talk with you about it. You have this image of me on how you want me to be. I am my own man, and I will run Reed Global the way I see fit, and do as I damn well please that suits my needs for my future. You can stand beside me, or you are free to retire, but you will not tell me what I can and cannot do any longer."

"Touché, my son. Are you ready to leave New York for California?"

"I'll let you know when I'm ready to leave."

"She's not coming back, Walker. The sooner you get that through your head, the sooner you will be able to move forward with Elizabeth. It is clear to everyone here tonight where you belong and who should be by your side."

"That's your one free pass, father. If you ever mention Reese's name again in my presence, I promise you that you will live to regret it." I turn and slam out of his study and out to the grounds. I need a fucking minute to myself to breathe. Sure it comes to everyone's surprise, even Elizabeth.

I only told one person my true passion, and it was Reese. In the short time we were together, she knew everything about me to the deepest depths of my core. I look up to the stars, and remember Georgia... making love to her under the Georgia sky, and wrapping ourselves up with each other. My buzzing phone knocks me out of my daydreaming, and I answer it.

No one is speaking, but I hear breathing on the other end. My heart hurts that it could be Reese. I am willing her to speak, but the line is still silent. I take a breath and speak for the both of us. "Reese, don't say anything, just listen, please. I don't know why you ran, but I love you and want you back. Please trust me enough to believe how much I love and want you. Look to the heart that I gave you, and feel my love. Come back to me baby, please."

Click....The line goes dead, and so does my heart. Dammit! I shatter my phone on the ground and then throw it out into the night sky. "Fuck, Fuck, Fuck!" I fall to my knees, and scream... "Reese! Why are you doing this to me? I love you, I fucking love you, and what do you do? You run from that love... Why?"

I am still on my knees, crying like a pathetic lovesick puppy. How the hell did I get here? Where the hell is she? And if she doesn't want me, then why the phone calls? Is she trying to pierce my broken heart even more? I truly believe at this moment that I have lost my love. I have done all I can to find her. Although I don't want to, this was never my choice. She took my choice away the moment she decided to leave me. I look up to the night sky once more, and say goodbye to Reese. I stagger up onto my feet and hear rustling sounds coming from the designer bushes out here in my mother's prized garden. Elizabeth reveals herself to me and slowly walks up to me.

"There you are. I couldn't find you anywhere. Are you okay?"

"I'm more than okay." I lied, but I have to start somewhere.

"I was wondering if you care to share another dance with me." She looks hopeful. I decide at that moment to give Elizabeth the one thing she wants... me. After my breakdown that I hope she didn't witness too much of, I make the choice to not be alone tonight. Elizabeth has offered herself up to me, time and time again, so now let's see if she really means it.

I take her in my arms and begin to kiss her behind her ear. She softly lets out moans of pleasure, as I continue to assault her neck. I cup her face and lose myself in her eyes. I kiss her passionately on her mouth, not giving her a chance to come up for air. Trying to get her breathing under control, she waits patiently for what I am about to say to her.

"I'm actually interested in another kind of dance…a more private one. Care to join me?" Her eyes brighten with my indecent proposal, and happily she entwines her hand into mine.

"I thought you would never ask. Lead the way"

Oh we do. As fast as our feet can take us. I'm going to fuck Reese Mitchell out of my head tonight, and give Elizabeth exactly what she has always wanted.

CHAPTER TWENTY-ONE

This changes everything...

WE NEVER SAID our goodbyes to our parents, nor my guests. They were enjoying my father's very expensive wine and champagne list, why spoil their fun? I led Elizabeth to my bedroom and locked the door behind us.

I forcefully pull her body toward me and crash my mouth down onto hers. She resists at first, and then welcomes my tongue in her mouth. I begin to remove her from her clothing. I am so fucking hard right now, being gentle is the last thing on my mind. Pushing her hands against my chest, I pull back and look at her with confused eyes. Dammit! Isn't this what she wants? She's only been offering herself up to me every chance she gets.

"What's wrong? Why are you stopping?"

"Walker, before we go any further, we need to make a few things clear between us."

"Us?" We are not an "us." We are just two friends that are about to fuck each other into my mattress for many hours. I say, "What's the problem, Elizabeth? Isn't this what you want? What you've always wanted? So, now I'm here and you stop me? I'm not

about to play some fucking school girl game with you, either you take your clothes off, and lay yourself down on that bed, or get the fuck out!"

Slap!

"What the hell? I swear that is the last time you ever raise your hand to me again!" I hurl myself at her and want to throw her down and take what she's promised me. I want to fuck her with my mouth until she is falling apart around me. I don't even recognize myself anymore! Who am I? What is happening to me?

Reeling my temper in, I fix myself a much needed drink. Elizabeth is shooting daggers at me with her eyes. Fuck! This was a mistake.

"I slapped you, because once again, you are behaving like an arrogant bastard that just thinks he can take whatever he wants. I want you to have me, Walker, I always have. But I am no whore, and you will not treat me like one."

"Do you think I want to hurt you like this, Elizabeth? You are the last person I want to hurt, but can't you see that I am broken inside? My appearance here tonight, and the speech I gave was just smoke and mirrors. My insides have been torn to shreds by a woman who I thought loved and wanted me. I can't even begin to tell you how that feels. This is why I've been drowning in scotch and wallowing in my pain, because it's all I have left of her. The hole she left in my heart. The way you are looking at me right now is what I've been trying to avoid. I don't want to hurt you."

"Then don't hurt me, Walker. Do you think for one second that it has been easy for me to listen to your cries of pain? I know how you feel, Walker, because it's exactly how I have felt every time I had to witness you with someone else. She's gone Walker, and I don't know why, but I'm here…I've always been here." With apprehension, Elizabeth softly strokes the stubble that lines my jaw. I cock my head to one side and welcome her touch. "Love me. Choose me. Make love to me. Me, Walker… Just me. I know I'm not the one you truly want, but I can be if you try. I have loved you my entire life, and you are my heart. Please let me into yours, and let's just see where it leads us. I know you don't feel like you deserve me, but you do. And I deserve you."

She falls to the floor and holds her head in her hands. Tears are now falling down her beautiful face. I can't bear to see the pain in her eyes and know I'm the one that has put it there. I bend down and kneel before her lifting her chin with my fingers. I wipe away her tears and taste the salt on her lips as I gently kiss them away.

Surrender...Submit...give in to your desire. I want her. She wants me. We need no more words...no more tears. It's only "us" in this room. I finally cast my own pain aside and give up myself willingly to her, even if it was for one night. Elizabeth is no whore. I would never think of her in that way. She is an angel that deserves to be wanted and cherished. A woman that you don't use for a quick fuck, she is a woman that you marry. My throbbing dick wanted hard, fast and penetrating sex. I was fighting against the tide to do the right thing by Elizabeth. Her submissiveness to do anything to please me was a force of will that I was sure to lose.

Elizabeth was everything a man would crave to have in a lover. She was perfect and nothing would have pleased our parents more if we ended up together. Elizabeth knew who my soul belonged to, but didn't care. She wanted me any way she can have me. I ached for Reese, my heart had been broken, and I needed to be close to another warm body. Elizabeth filled that void for me. Alcohol masked my pain, and all I wanted to do was forget.

I led Elizabeth over to my bed and slowly began to remove her clothing. *Sweet Jesus! She was beautiful.* I quickly made strides to remove my clothes, and I hovered above her, as she gazed into my eyes. She was all over me. Elizabeth began kissing me while trailing her tongue down my neck and onto my chest. I let her touch me as my thoughts drifted and fantasized about Reese. I hate myself for going there again, but I can't help it. While cupping her now exposed pussy, and getting herself aroused, she was wet and ready for me. I flipped her over and onto the bed. We tore at each other's remaining articles of clothing that we had on. She was ready and waited for me to take her.

Her body hungered for me, she was moaning out cries of pleasure as I entered her. She was so tight; I was not gentle in my love making with Elizabeth. I picked up my pace and pounded into her until I climaxed and fell on top of her. I pressed my forehead into hers and kissed her, I didn't want to be a total asshole. Elizabeth deserved more than I just gave her, but I was just too lost to care.

Waking up the next morning, I felt warm hands across my chest. For a moment, I thought Reese returned to me. *I have to stop torturing myself with false hope.* I damn well knew who was lying next to me. I fucked my best friend last night. *What the hell was I thinking?* I already know the answer to that. My dick was my navigator last night, and it was aimed directly at her very inviting pussy. Yeah…I'm a bastard. I turned to see Elizabeth sleeping soundly. She looked beautiful. Why she wanted me, I don't think I will ever understand. I gently kissed her forehead before untangling myself from her embrace. I tried to be quiet and padded off into the bathroom. Why did I feel guilty?

I feel like I have betrayed my lover and hurt another. I scorched my skin with hot water, washing away Elizabeth's scent off my body. The curtain opened and Elizabeth was asking for entrance. I nodded, and she stepped in to join me. It was obvious what Elizabeth wanted, she knelt down before me, and I fucked her mouth with my cock. She took me all the way in as I grasped my hands on the sides of her head. I leaned back and enjoyed Elizabeth taking control. "God! You feel so fucking good. I'm going to come any second now. If you don't want me to explode in your mouth, then stop."

Not backing down, Elizabeth cupped my balls, and I spurted hot semen down her throat. She smiled and tilted her head back in pleasure. She had a wickedness about her this morning. Her dominance surprised me, but who the hell was I kidding? What guy wouldn't like that? I took it all from her, as she willingly gave it. Deciding that I wasn't finished with her quite yet, I wrapped her legs around my waist and took her again. Elizabeth was a screamer! Who knew? I silenced her cries of pleasure with my mouth until she broke away and bit down on my shoulder. *Fuck!* She bites too!

She was insatiable. Three rounds of hot sex, and she was finally sated. I had to clear my head, or I was going to be inside of her for the rest of the day. I took out the Jag and sped away from my parent's home.

I was sending Elizabeth all the wrong signals. I shouldn't have let her do that to me, but I was not thinking clearly at the time. All I could think about was Reese and wondering why she left and where the hell she was. I was using Elizabeth and she was letting me. When I wasn't drowning in scotch, I was fucking Elizabeth; she gave herself to me anytime I wanted it. I felt sick about how I was treating her, but at the same time I didn't want to be alone. Elizabeth didn't seem to mind how our friendship turned into friends with benefits. If she did, she never said. We had been photographed together several times following my graduation party, and then it was May. My mother pleaded with me to walk with my graduating class. I had paparazzi following me all over the city, and they were here today in droves. I was after all, the new CEO of Reed Global, I had a beautiful woman on my arm, and to the world we were the new "It" couple. In print we looked like the perfect couple in love, which pleased our families to no end, especially my father.

The ceremony went off without a hitch, and then I was hit with a question that I didn't see coming. "Mr. Reed... Mr. Reed, over here, sir. Isn't it true a few months back, you were seeing an Elite model? What happened?"

I wanted to rip his camera out of his hands and beat him with it. I of course couldn't do that. Cosmopolitan's May issue had come out days earlier, and I had forgotten that I had ordered a subscription to the magazine because my woman was gracing its cover. I cleared my throat, and simply answered the reporter. "I don't make comments on my personal life, but thank you for coming out today." He was not satisfied with my answers, and asked several more of me, it was then that Ralston came to my rescue and hurried me out of there and into my waiting car.

"Thanks" I muttered to him.

"Sir, now that you are so high profile, you will need a security team."

"I'm well aware of that, and I have it covered." I answer him curtly. I never liked Ralston. He works for my father, not for me.

CHAPTER TWENTY-TWO

Make a choice...

THE FOLLOWING WEEK after officially graduating NYU, I traveled to California. Along with my father we took some meetings, and met with my new staff. After my night spent with Elizabeth, and the morning that followed, I was exhausted. Lying in bed naked, and entwined with each other, I was happy to put some space between us. The last thing I wanted to do was fuck her and leave her, but I already knew what Elizabeth had wanted. She wants more. She has been patiently waiting for me to give her the green light. I knew I needed to talk with her, but it would have to wait. I was here in California for work.

While walking the path that led to the entrance of our new building, I felt something weird… a presence that literally felt like a barrier that I couldn't walk through. I haven't felt this strong presence for quite a while now, not since New York. I was confused by the familiar pull that my entire body was now reacting to. My father nearly collided into my back when I stopped walking. For a minute, I had thought he was almost alarmed by my actions.

"Walker, what's wrong?" He didn't understand what I was doing. I didn't know myself, but I had to find out.

"Quiet!" I shouted at him, and he obediently did. I tried to center in on the magnetic pull that had me rooted to where I stood. I scanned the area, and saw nothing. This is insane. Whatever it was, it's gone now, leaving me feeling five shades of foolish. I shrugged it off and began walking toward the entrance.

My father was not following me now. I turn to him. "Are you coming?" I curtly ask him. My father's expression that he wore didn't elude me, but I was already late and needed to get upstairs to my office.

He snapped his phone shut. "Walker, I need to take care of a matter of urgency, will you excuse me for a moment?"

"What is it? Can't you handle it once we get inside?"

"This will not wait. This is personal. You need not to concern yourself over it."

Now I am concerned. "Is it mother?"

"No! Of course not. I just have something that needs my attention. I'll be in as soon as I can."

"Have it your way, Father, but I need you inside when you finish with whatever you are hiding behind that smirk of yours."

"Walker, can't you ever see anything behind your hate for me?"

"It's not hate, Father. I just know you all too well, and I can see clearly what others can't. Whatever you are plotting in that devious mind of yours will not be welcomed up in there. Do I make myself clear?

"CRYSTAL." MY SON gestures to our new building standing behind him. He leaves me standing there. My son's displeasure of me is evident. He makes no secret in hiding it. He never looks back, and he quickly enters the building. The atrium of Reed Global has been designed in glass panels. The expansive welcoming area is filled with exotic flowers and plants. I lose sight of him once he is beyond the bay of elevators.

Dammit! Walker, is right. I am barely hanging on by a thread, and keeping him from discovering my betrayal. I now need to deal with Ms. Mitchell. How Ralston prevented her from calling out to Walker is a miracle. Walker stopped in his tracks, though, as if he'd seen her, but that would have been impossible. Plus, he went upstairs, so I'm sure he hadn't noticed her. I dodged a bullet, this I know. If Walker would have discovered Ms. Mitchell, it would have been over for me. He would have shown me no mercy.

Who am I kidding? I don't deserve it after what I did to her. I dismiss my moment of weakness. I can't have guilt clouding my judgment. I must once again show her the ruthless side she knows me to be.

I make my way over to the now silenced Ms. Mitchell. "Well, well, well. You are the last person I expected to see, but here you are."

My man, Ralston, has his hand over her mouth, preventing her from screaming. I look right into her eyes, and instruct her not to scream, and he will let her go. She blinks at me, and he releases his hands from her mouth and body. Once he does, the feisty Ms. Mitchell delivers a kick right to his groin, making Ralston fall to his knees in pain.

"You piece of shit! Don't touch me!" Now she turns to me, and I caution her that striking at me would not be a smart decision. She steps back to catch her breath and hold her protruding baby bump. Once again, I feel the shame piercing my heart. She's carrying my grandchild…Walker's child. I am in hell. No turning back now.

"Well Ms. Mitchell, I never thought I would see you again. What are you doing here? Need more money, perhaps?" I didn't want to travel down this road again with this poor girl, especially since Walker was so close to marrying Elizabeth, and I would finally be free of the deal I had made with her father. Walker would never really know the part I played in all of this. I had to be forceful once again. I had to scare the living shit out of her. I was doing it for her and for me.

"You know I never cashed your check, I want nothing from you, ever! You can't keep me from Walker, I love him, and I know he loves me. I am going into that building and I am going to expose you for the manipulator and liar you are! You son of a bitch."

I grab her arm, and then Ralston re-joins me. "You will do no such thing, little girl. I meant what I said to you the last time we met. I am a man of my word, and I will destroy you if you force my hand."

"What if I told you that my family knows everything, and they are willing to stand up against you, and your threats? We are not afraid, and we will fight you. Walker will be the one destroying you when he finds out all that you've done to me, and to us. I am carrying his child, and he is going to know today."

"The hell he is." I grit my teeth. She steps back in fear.

I take out my phone, and begin to dial a number. Her eyes never leave mine. She begins to break down, she is losing her fight. I've already won this battle, but I still go in for the kill.

"Miles, Reed here. Ms. Mitchell seems to have resurfaced. You know what to do." I snap my phone shut in front of her face.

"No, don't Mr. Reed!" Please don't hurt my family."

"Oh, Ms. Mitchell, but I thought you were ready to fight me with all that you have, isn't that what you said?"

"I love your son. Please let me go to him. I can't live without him." She once again drops to her knees, and I have completely destroyed this precious girl before me. I hate myself, but it has to be done.

"Ms. Mitchell, he has moved on without you. Please do yourself a favor and leave here today and never look back. It truly is your only choice." She unsteadily stays on the ground, and holds her growing belly.

"You can't keep us apart forever, Mr. Reed. Love does conquer all, and it is the strongest bond between two people. I know he still loves me, I can feel him even though he's not with me. It doesn't matter how many women he beds, I know I'm the one that holds his heart."

She shows me her locket, and I tear it from her neck, leaving her to gasp. I shove the necklace in my pocket. "Not anymore, Ms. Mitchell. Not anymore."

"What are you doing? Give me my necklace back, please, please Mr. Reed." She is still on her knees while begging me to show her an ounce of humanity, but I ignore her and walk toward my building. Never looking back at the shattered girl, I try with all my resolve to forget the piercing sounds of her painful cries. *Go to hell, Phillip Reed, Go to hell!* If she only knew…I'm already there.

I make my way up to the executive offices and meet the death glare from my very angry son.

"Where the hell have you been? Our lawyers have been waiting for more than an hour." Clearly my son is furious with me, but I cover with another lie.

"I told you, son, it was personal and couldn't wait. I'm here now, calm yourself Walker, and let's begin. Thank you, gentlemen, for your patience. Now, where are we?"

Walker doesn't say another word to me, and we continue on with our business at hand. I watch him take charge of the room. It is a glorious sight to take in. This is what I have always wanted for my son. He is a natural. He has easily taken to his new role as I always thought he would. Hours later, we leave Reed Global in silence. Walker is swiftly walking to our waiting car, as I glance around the property. Ms. Mitchell is nowhere to be seen. I have my men on her anyway. They would have alerted me if she would have tried again to gain access to Walker.

"What's the matter with you today?" Walker barks at me, as he hands off his briefcase to our driver. "You have been distracted all day. What is it, father? Did I not meet all your expectations with the board?"

Thinking quickly to calm him. I lied…again. "Walker, you were brilliant today. I couldn't have been more proud of you."

"Then what is it? We are under enough pressure, and I don't

need you distracted. I watched you zone out a few times during the presentation. Let me be clear, that type of behavior will not be tolerated."

"I understand. I am no exception to the rule. It won't happen again."

"Good. See that it doesn't."

We board the company jet, and it flies us home back to New York. Silence and distance is between us. What did I expect? This is what I wanted. My son...master of the boardroom. The mogul I groomed him to be. The only difference is that he has kindness and love in him that I never possessed. He's just lashing out right now because he is still hurting over his loss. I have to believe he has enough strength to move on and forget about her. He has to! For both our sakes.

Walker needs to pack his remaining things from his penthouse apartment. He will retain his residence in New York, while also living in California. We held onto our New York properties for many reasons; our hub is on two coasts, so it would only make sense for him to keep his home. It's our building after all, but I would have thought he would want to find a new place since it held many sad memories for him, but he wouldn't hear of it. He said he wasn't ready, and this I didn't push him on. I've done enough to hurt him, why take his only place of solace away too?

My son has already begun taking Reed Global in a different direction. He is after all in charge. This will be a difficult transition for me to adjust to, but I know my son. He is not the ruthless bastard like I am. I am still in the game. I just need to be patient with him and continue to lead him directly to Elizabeth, and away from Ms. Mitchell.

After what feels like an excruciating flight, we finally arrive at J.F.K. Airport. Traveling with my father is always taxing on my nerves. He infuriated me today with his disappearing act. As much as I appear to be prepared and focused, I still need my father's knowledge to guide me. I almost didn't recognize myself today. I have never been so short tempered in all of my life. I can't wait to return to the comforts of my home, and forget about this day. My father and I exit our plane and make our way to our waiting car. He still looks apprehensive to me.

"Are you okay?" I finally ask him. This time my question is calmer. This is not like him to behave this way.

"I'm fine Walker, just tired. To be separated from your mother all these weeks has taken a toll on me." For once, I don't lie.

"Very well then." As my son exits the car. I let out my breath that I was holding.

NOT EXACTLY ENJOYING coming home to an empty apartment, I do welcome the quiet away from Phillip. He was definitely off his game today. I feel it deep in my core that he is hiding something, but what? I decide not to stress over it any more tonight. I begin shutting down the apartment when my doorbell rings.

"Hi, I wasn't expecting to see you tonight." I'm taken by surprise to see Elizabeth, standing on the threshold of my home. I thought she was still out of town with her father. She was designing a new home and office space that her father purchased out in Arizona. He wants to eventually retire out there with his wife, but for now he is using the house to vacation during his off time. The sight of her makes me smile. I take her coat, and she walks into my arms wrapping herself around me. She's shaking.

"What's the matter, baby?" I shock myself at my choice of words that I use with her, taking her by surprise as well.

"I'm pregnant, Walker." She breaks away from me, and sits down on the sofa. I'm completely thrown by what she has just said, so I ask her again.

"What did you just say?"

"I think you heard me the first time," she says through her tears.

"How can this be? Elizabeth, we used protection." *Oh shit! Not our first time back in the Hamptons on the weekend of my party.*

Fuck! How irresponsible can I be? This is the worst excuse for manners; I've gotten my best friend/lover pregnant.

Trying to calm myself and her down, I go and join her on the couch. "Elizabeth, are you sure?" She looks at me with the expression that says it all, *Are you kidding me?*

"Is it mine?" I brace myself for the slap that I know is coming, but she doesn't hit me, she just breaks down and cries.

"Yes, it's yours, Walker. You are the only man that I have ever been with."

My heart hurts. *Another virgin? FUCK!* Now she is carrying my child. My child is growing inside of her, and here I sit questioning her as if she was some gold digger after my money. This is Elizabeth, for **Fuck Sake!** Hurting me would be the last thing on her mind.

"I only came here to tell you about the baby, and the decision that I've made."

"Which is what? Terminate the pregnancy? Hell no, Elizabeth, I will never allow that to happen." I almost grab and shake her, but pull back my hands.

"I would never do that to our baby, Walker. How could you even postulate such a thing? I'm keeping this baby, and I will raise my child on my own. My parents already know. Of course they want you to do the right thing by me, but I will not force you into anything you are not ready for."

"But it's *our* child."

"What?"

"I said, it's our child, and I don't expect you to raise him or her on your own." Elizabeth turns to me with new hope in her eyes. "Can you please just give me some time to absorb this news? This was the last thing I was expecting to hear."

"Of course, and just you so know, this shocked me too. I love you Walker, and I know in my heart we can be happy, if you allow your heart to open and accept my love. I'll take you anyway I can have you, but I need your promise of commitment, and I need to believe that you will try. If you can't at least give me that, then we have nothing else to discuss." She grabs her coat and purse, and quickly leaves my home. I remain sitting as I watch her go.

This is not how I imagined my future to be. I was supposed to be marrying Reese, and building a future with her. Having kids with her... not Elizabeth! The weeks following my weekend with Elizabeth, I finally severed ties with Reese's grandparents. Lila did call a few times, but with no information on Reese. Freddy completely shut me out and never returned one of my phone calls, and then there was that mystery caller. I never did find out who called me that night. I traced the number back to a burner phone, with an unknown location. I had no choice but to carry on with my life, and hope Reese was doing the same. I couldn't handle looking at her beautiful face on anymore magazine covers, so I buried it away along with my feelings for Reese. The life I had and wanted to have with Reese was gone. I now needed to decide how I would go on without her occupying my thoughts twenty four hours a day. I had Elizabeth to think about and a child on its way.

A few phone calls between us, I still hadn't given Elizabeth the answer she wanted to hear. I was working fourteen hour work days, and flying back and forth to California and New York. My father was relentless and her father no better. Our mothers had our wedding in place, all they needed was for me and Elizabeth to show up. They were once again steering the course of my life, and if I wanted it different, I would have to man up and take my control back. Was I ready for this? To be a husband and father?

Sitting in my office, and preparing for my next meeting. Henry Townsend barges through my door, as my man Stephen restrains him.

"I'm sorry, sir, he got past me."

Looking up from my computer. "It's quite all right, Stephen, let him go."

Now I am coming face to face with Henry Townsend, and his wrath. "You asshole! How could you hurt my baby girl this way? I just left her with her mother in tears and crying over you. A man that won't commit to a woman who loves him and is carrying his child. What do you have to say for yourself, son? My daughter is devastated, and is on her way back to California. She no longer can live here and wait for you to grow up."

"What? Elizabeth is leaving? What the fuck is wrong with the women in my life? One leaves me without ever telling me why and the other is having my baby, and is also leaving me! With not one word between us? Well, hell no! I will not let another person walk away from me." I realize I am screaming out loud, and now Henry is smiling at me. "What the hell are you looking at? And what pray tell is so funny?" I shout at him.

Proudly looking back at me. He says… "I'm looking at the man I know you to be. I'm laughing now because you have made me very proud, and I know you will make my daughter and grandchild very happy. I'm looking at my son-in-law. Now go after her, Walker, before it's too late."

He bear hugs me and leaves my office. I feel as if my limbs are betraying me, and I can't move from where I stand. I call out to Stephen to bring the car around. I have a plane to stop.

"Stephen, please drive faster. I don't care how many traffic laws we have to break, I can't let Elizabeth get on that plane." She promised to give me time to sort this out, and now she thinks leaving me is the best way to solve our issues. I know I haven't been the ideal boyfriend for her, but we have been better since the Hamptons. I've been better. Trying to move on from loving Reese takes all my discipline and control. When Elizabeth told me that she was pregnant, and with *my child*, something inside of me shifted. I don't know what it is, but it felt scary and exciting all at the same time.

I'm not the average twenty two year old by any means. I have just been appointed CEO of one of the largest development companies in the world. I should be on top of the world, and yet I'm chasing down the mother of my child that is running away from me. This is why I didn't want to pursue anything with Elizabeth. We have been friends for far too long and hurting Elizabeth was never an option, but it's all I seem to do.

How will I know I can even be a good father? Phillip Reed wasn't exactly the ideal role model for me. I can say without a doubt that I will never be like him. I will love my child, and always put him or her first. If I didn't know it already, I'm already in love with my baby. I have to try to convince Elizabeth to give me another chance. I know in time I can make her happy. I've always known that she deserves more, but now she's carrying my child? I will never be able to let her go.

"How much longer until we reach the airport, Stephen?"

"We're just about there, sir. I'll drop you off in front." Please let me make it. We arrive at J.F.K Airport, and I run through the busy terminal. I have her information from her father. I scan the crowd, and there is no sign of Elizabeth.

"Excuse me, miss?"

"Yes, sir, Can I help you."

"I hope so. Flight 3456 to Los Angeles, has it departed yet?"

"Yes, sir. Five minutes ago. Were you scheduled to be on that flight? I can put you on a stand-by list for later this evening."

"No, that won't be necessary."

She's gone? I missed her by only a few minutes. I can't believe she got on the plane without talking to me first. Why Elizabeth? After all I've been through these last few months, how could you just leave me? I feel sick and utterly broken again. Just when I thought I was beginning to put my life back together, Elizabeth blows it wide open. I see Stephen approaching me. He figures by my demeanor that we're too late.

"Sir, I can call your pilot and prepare the jet for you."

I can't even think right now. Do I chase her all the way to California? Wait to hear from her? My head is spinning, and I don't know where to start. I run my fingers through my hair, and rub my face in frustration. My mind is returning to how elated her father was when I declared that I would go after his daughter and fight for her.

This is what our parents have wanted all along, for me to marry Elizabeth and build a future with her in California. Now she's left me, and I have no course of action to take.

I gesture to Stephen to go, and as we walk, I see her! She didn't get on the plane, but where is she coming out from? I slowly walk toward her, not wanting to alarm her with my presence. She doesn't look well; her face is pale.

"Elizabeth?" she slowly turns around and her tears begin to fall down her ashen face. My heart hurts. *This is my fault.* In two strides toward her, I have her in my arms. She falls against my chest and begins to cry uncontrollably. Stephen is looking at me with concern. I gesture to him to grab her bags from her. As I walk her over to a chair, I kneel before her, taking her hands in mine.

"I'm so sorry, Elizabeth. I'm ashamed on how I've behaved. Please don't leave me, let me try to be the man you need, and the father to our child. I won't know what I will do if I lose you both."

"I'm sorry. I should be the one that feels ashamed. It's been days since I told you about the baby, and I was feeling lost, confused and so hurt by your distance. If I didn't get sick before departure, I would have gotten on that plane." She weeps some more.

"I would have followed you." She looks up at me as if she can't believe what I just said. "Elizabeth, please come home with me now. I want you to stay with me."

"For how long, Walker? You can't keep playing with my heart and my feelings, it's not fair and I have to protect our child now. It's not just you and me anymore." She was making perfect sense, and she was right.

"Walker, what did she have that I didn't? Why is it so hard for you to let go of her? I've loved you for years, and you never gave me a second glance, and when you finally did, it was only to heal what someone else broke in you. It's not fair, and I can't be what you need or want me to be for you Walker. I'll be your friend, but nothing more. I'll take care of our child, and you can go and be the master of the universe and run Reed Global."

Can she shatter me anymore? "No Elizabeth, you're wrong. You will not just send me away, and not expect me to fight for you, our baby, and us."

"Don't you see, Walker? We are not an 'us.' We never were. Please let me go. I hope you find what you are looking for someday, because it's not me, and it's about time I finally realize it." She gets up and leaves me where I have knelt before her.

I call out to her. "Elizabeth!" She stops, and turns to look at me. I'm still on my knees before her, as I pull out a box from my pocket. She gasps at the sight of the diamond before her.

"Elizabeth, please give me a chance to love you like you deserve. Please let me be a father to our child. If you say 'yes' to me today, I promise I will never hurt you again." I rise from the floor, and lift her chin so she can look at my eyes. "I promise to be committed to you and our child for the rest of my days. I promise to be a good husband, father, and all you need me to be. Please give me this second chance to prove to you that I can honor these promises, and love you. Please, Elizabeth, I need you, don't leave me." I wrap my arms around her and kiss her forehead and wet cheeks, and my lips find hers. She is slowly resisting and breaking down. She loves me, this I know, but she is afraid to trust me again. On the life of our child, I promise I will never hurt them.

Now looking up at me, "You truly promise, Walker? You want a marriage and family with me, and only me?"

God, she's beautiful and so precious. She has every right to doubt me. I kiss her once more and I tell her the one thing she desperately needs to hear from me.

"Elizabeth, I love you. I love our child. I want you to stay with me...forever."

"Yes, Walker, I will marry you!" I sweep her up into my arms and twirl her around the terminal. I place the ring on her finger, and kiss it as it is secured in place. I take her hand in mine and whisper in her ear, "Let's go home."

Following the weeks after we publicly announced our engagement, paparazzi were following Elizabeth throughout the city. I had hired extra security for her, and then decided to move her to my parents' estate in the Hamptons. We would be getting married in a few days, and I just needed to tie up some loose ends in the city before we move to California.

I found myself sitting alone in my huge penthouse apartment. I was surrounded by memories of my time spent here with Reese. I promised myself and Elizabeth that I would lay to rest the old ghosts of my past and not re-visit them again. I remember what she asked me the day at the airport. What does Reese have that she didn't?

I never answered Elizabeth. I don't even think I could if I wanted to. Reese was like no other person that I ever met in my life. She lit something up in me that no other woman has ever done. She was a breath of fresh air that blew into my life, and after seeing her that day in the library, I knew I had to have her. I'll never understand why she left me. Visions of Reese still haunt me. I loved her then, and I love her now, but I owe it to Elizabeth and our child to be what they need me to be. To promise "forever" to Elizabeth easily was spoken from my lips to her ears. They were nearly the same words I used to pledge my love for Reese. Now everything has changed. Reese is gone. Elizabeth is here and carrying my child.

I meant what I said to Reese when I gave her the locket. She owns my heart...forever. I know I have to make room for Elizabeth in my heart. She deserves better, but I'm a selfish man and I will not let that last part of Reese go. My child is growing inside of Elizabeth, and as her belly grows, so does my love for my baby and its mother. Before leaving, I walk over to my mantle, and take down the one picture that has been with me since Reese left.

It was taken while we were in Georgia. She's smiling at me as my hand caresses her face. I run my fingers over the picture frame, closing my eyes to feel what I felt on this day spent with her. I place a kiss to her face, and wipe away my one tear that falls down my cheek. I place our picture in my wall safe that now joins her ring.

The ring that I was to give her, to have our lives join as one. I repeatedly tried to return this ring to her grandmother, but she always refused, even after she heard about me marrying Elizabeth. Lila believed that one day our paths would cross again and our love would still be alive within us both. I don't know how true that is, but I wasn't going to argue with one of the wisest women I have ever had the honor of knowing.

I locked the safe, and took one last look around the room. Taking in some slow breaths, my heart was beginning to ache with what I was about to do. If I was ever going to have another chance at happiness, I knew what I had to say that my heart has been battling me not to. My thoughts betray me, and my words begin to feel like hot burning oil scorching my throat.

"Goodbye, Reese Mitchell."

CHAPTER TWENTY-THREE

This I promise you...

I MARRIED ELIZABETH Townsend in front of our family and the few close friends we had between us. We both agreed on a simple ceremony, despite what our mothers were planning. When we threatened to elope, that quieted them. Elizabeth did get her dream wedding, but it was on her terms. She looked exquisite as her father escorted her down the beach path that led to me waiting for her. She promised no tears today. Today it was our new beginning for the life that we were to have together as husband and wife. I meant every promise I made to her. The look in her eyes tells me that she believes me, trusting me with her fragile heart.

Her father, Henry, lifted her veil, kissed her cheek, and placed her hand in mine. "Be happy today, tomorrow, and for the rest of your lives." I nodded at her father, and he turned to join his wife. Elizabeth winked at me. We listened to the reverend recite the vows for us to say to one another. Elizabeth never faltered, and not one tear fell. Her radiant smile spoke volumes on how happy she was.

Before he pronounced us husband and wife, I did something that even shocked me. I dropped to one knee and placed a kiss on my wife's belly, and whispered to my child, "I love you. I am not only becoming a husband today to your mom, but 'we' become a family. I can't wait to hold you in my arms and kiss your mommy for giving me 'you' and making me the happiest man in the world."

Well, that did it. My bride let her tears fall, but I knew they were happy ones. I wiped them away and waited to officially kiss my wife. He looked at the two of us and pronounced us not only husband and wife, but today we became a family.

"You may kiss your bride."

"You better believe it." I smile proudly. I took Elizabeth as close as I could and poured every bit of love and emotion into my kiss. Whispering over and over again how happy she has made me here today. We turned to greet the crowd, and we were cheered on as we made our way down the path.

Hand in hand, we were greeted by our family and friends wishing us well. I kept looking over to my wife, looking for any telltale sign of uncertainty, but all I saw was love. She was truly happy, and what I had planned next would truly complete our day. For days I did research on finding the perfect song to be played for our first dance as husband and wife.

My mother had something already chosen, but I told her no. I would choose the song for Elizabeth, a song that would forever show her that my commitment to her and our child were true. When I listened to these lyrics, I knew I had found our song.

After listening to toasts delivered by our fathers, it was now time for mine to my bride. I took to the microphone and looked right into her eyes.

"Thank you for being here and helping us celebrate our special day. I know my wife is waiting with bated breath on the song that I have chosen for us to dance to for the first time as a married couple. The road that led Elizabeth and I here was not always an easy one traveled. My wife saved me in more ways that I can ever thank her for. I was drowning, as she held out her hand to pull me to safety, and into the comforts of her love. She patiently waited for me to be the man she always knew I could be, and when I was ready to do so, she gave me the greatest gift a man could ever receive. She gave me our child, and then just to show off, she accepted my marriage proposal."

My eyes never left hers, as she smiled and laughed. She placed her hands on her stomach and blew me a kiss.

"Elizabeth, I hope you like the song that I have chosen for us. I hope it tells you what you truly mean to me, and how happy you have made me. I love you."

I stepped down, took her in my arms, as the band began to play…"This I promise you." I held her in my arms. Her body moved easily with mine, as I sang the very song that says it all for me.

"My love, here I stand before you. I am yours now. From this moment on, take my hand. My love, here I stand before you. I am yours now. From this moment on, take my hand. Only you can stop me shaking. We'll share forever. This I promise you.

When I look in your eyes, all of my life is before me. I'm not running anymore, because I already know I'm home. With every beat of my heart, I give you my love completely. My darling. This I promise you.

My love, I can feel your heartbeat, as we dance now. Closer than before, don't let go, don't let go. I can almost cry now. This is forever. I make this vow to you. When I look in your eyes, all of my life feels before me, and I'm not running anymore. I already know I'm home."

With every beat of my heart, I give you my love completely. My darling, this I promise you. My darling, this I promise you. This I promise you, oh I promise you, promise you. This I promise you…"

Our song had ended, and Elizabeth placed her hand on my heart, as I kissed her tears away.

"I love you, Walker, so much. Thank you for making all my dreams come true."

I held her in my arms and closed my eyes to just feel her love wash over me, and for a brief second, I remembered Reese. *Damn my betraying thoughts!* I owed it to Elizabeth to put her and our child first, but once again pangs of guilt were riddling through me. I imagined this day to be very different, and my bride to be Reese. I believed that if you stepped out into the street without looking, you may get hit by an oncoming car.

To believe in destiny and the universe, well that was a hard pill to swallow. I always relied on facts before me, not what might have been. To say that everything happens for a reason, well I'm not sure I believe that either. All I know is what I have here today: my wife, my child, my future. This is what I know to be true.

EPILOGUE

Goodbye my friend...

IT WAS TOUCH and go for a while there. His cord was tangled around his neck and the doctors were unsure if he was deprived of oxygen. My wife was on the operating table. She was declared brain dead after suffering a massive stroke. Elizabeth was never going to recover, never knowing our child. Life was incredibly unfair and cruel. I held her hand as I listened to her breaths being controlled by a machine. While the doctors worked on our son, I leaned into my wife's ear.

"I am so sorry this happened to you, and to us. I never thought I would be doing this without you. How can I do this without you? I will never be able to thank you for this incredible gift you have given me, our son. I promise you that I will be the best father I can be, and always tell our son about you. You were my lifeline when I was drowning. Thank you for loving me, Elizabeth."

I said my goodbyes to my wife and friend. She deserved so much better than half of a man who loved someone else. I kissed her forehead and was startled by the sound of a newborn crying. Our son made it and was screaming at the top of his lungs. I never heard a more beautiful sound in all of my life. The nurse brought him over to me. My hands were shaking. I was afraid to touch him. The nurse led me out of the room where the doctors could now finish up with Elizabeth.

I sat down in a rocking chair and was given my son to hold. Jackson looked just like me when I was a baby. His hair was dark, and he had my nose. He had stopped crying, and he wrapped his finger around mine. No turning back now, I was hooked. My son had captured my heart with one simple touch. His eyes were so bright, they matched his mothers. I would have to tell him one day about her. How do you explain why she's not here to raise him? It was my job to be mother and father to him, but how? Jackson was examined by a team of doctors. I spared no expense when it came to my son and wife.

He was perfectly healthy and could go home with me tomorrow. After our son was settled into the nursery, I was approached by a transplant team.

Elizabeth's organs needed to be harvested, time was of the essence. I needed to make a decision on what to do. She never told me she was an organ donor. Although she suffered a stroke, her organs were still viable, but would eventually shut down. How could I make this decision on my own? Her parents had left New York and settled in Arizona. I'm all alone out here and I need my wife, I need Elizabeth to show me the way. It wasn't supposed to be like this. How can after everything we've been through, this right here be the ending of our story? I collapsed onto the floor and wept like I have never done in my life. My child was depending on me now, and Elizabeth would have wanted me to be strong.

She had been complaining of headaches in the last trimester of her pregnancy. Her doctors assured us that sometimes this is normal, and Elizabeth showed no other symptoms to raise any red flags. Right after arriving in California, I threw myself into work, and running the business with my vision and plans for its future. Elizabeth created a home for us, paying attention to every last detail. Every room she decorated spoke volumes on how she could make a room inviting and warm. We chose our home together, and vowed to fill it always with love… and the sounds of many children. I knew once she gave me my son or daughter, how could I not want more to fill this large home.

We were both only children, and it can be very lonely growing up, especially in our circle. While our parents were close friends, it was expected for their children to be close as well. Elizabeth followed me everywhere I went, until finally I pulled her pony tail. I was hoping she would get mad and not bother me again, but not Elizabeth, she didn't cry. She pulled my hair, and I was the one shrieking. She wouldn't release my shaggy head of hair until I apologized to her. Once I did, we laughed and her smile lit up like the sun. From that day forward, Elizabeth and I became best friends.

Now as I agonize on what to do, my best friend is gone. She has unselfishly consented to donate her organs to another life in need. This is the person that I have always known her to be. She puts the needs of others before her own. I lifted my mentally drained body from off the floor, and heard wailing voices from the other side of the door. It was her parents, Henry and Gail. They took one look at me, and knew that their daughter was gone. Henry caught his wife in his arms. They held on to each other and screamed… "No! Not our Elizabeth."

Her father took me in his arms and wept on my shoulder. I had nothing to give back, but I'm sorry. My wife is dead, and my newborn son barely survived. In a matter of a few hours, the life that I had known and lived happily had completely changed. The sound of the machines breathed life into my wife now.

"Where is she? Where is our daughter?" Henry asked through his tears.

"She's still up in the O.R. Henry, Gail, did you know that Elizabeth was an organ donor?" The look on their faces tell me no. Apparently, she has been for several years now. Her new California license says the same as her New York one. The transplant team is on standby and waiting on my answer for consent. Elizabeth wanted this. I don't know why she never mentioned it to me, but they need an answer. Time is running out to harvest her organs."

"You are her husband, Walker. You consent to what your wife would have wanted. Can I ask about our grandchild? Is he okay?"

"He's beautiful, Henry, just beautiful."

"Can we see him? He's all we've got left." Her mother weeps in her husband's arms.

"Gail, Henry, you will always be part of his life. Elizabeth will live on through our son, and he's going to need his grandparents in his life. You are amazing people, and our son will always love you."

Just then the doors burst open, and my father makes his presence known, barking out orders and demanding information. I've taken all I can take, I'm not ready to go round and round with Phillip Reed right now. My mother is crying and consoling her friend. My father walks up to me and gives me a half hug.

"I'm so very sorry for your loss, my son. Is there anything we can do for you?" *Yeah, you can give my wife back.*

"No, father, there is nothing you can do for me. I need some time alone if you don't mind."

I turn away from them, and head to the nursery. I need to see my son. I need to hold him, and feel him against my skin. He is the one thing that can get me through this nightmare I'm living right now. The nurse buzzes me in, and I put on the necessary gown that I need to wear in here. I wash my hands over and over again until I'm satisfied that I'm clean. The older grey haired nurse squeezes my shoulders gently and tells me that it's okay to be nervous, he won't break.

How did she know this is one of my fears? He truly is all I have left of Elizabeth. I must always put him first above everything else in my life. I gaze into his beautiful brown eyes as I make many promises to him. He coos softly in my arms, as my tears fall.

I rock him gently and my mind drifts to Elizabeth and me just hours ago, asleep in our bed. She gently nudged me to wake, but I was out of it. I had just put in a fourteen hour work day and was completely exhausted. We had dinner together, and then I retired for the evening. Elizabeth joined me a short while after. She didn't show any signs of alarm. *Did she, and I was too oblivious to notice?* No! No matter how hard I worked, I always made sure her every need was met before taking care of my own.

How did we get here? We were asleep in our bed, and her water broke. I woke and sprang from our bed. Elizabeth was fearless, she simply got up, changed into fresh clothes, and reached for my hand.

"This is it. We get to meet our son, Walker. I love you so much, and I hope he looks like you."

"I love you too, and I only want him to be healthy and of course look like his beautiful mother." She smiles at me. I am so in love with her.

"Well, let's go meet our son." My wife was beaming. I couldn't help but be happy at this moment. I was about to become someone's father. The feeling felt so surreal to me. I kept looking over to Elizabeth for any signs of pain she may have been experiencing, but all I saw was her smile.

After we checked in to the hospital, we were greeted by her doctor. The phone calls have been made to our families, and Elizabeth's parents were on their way. I was sure to be seeing my father soon enough. He had been out here in California since I slowly eased into my new position at Reed Global. It hasn't been the power struggle I anticipated it would be with my father, but so far he has let me stand on my own. I was holding Elizabeth's hands while watching the monitor beep, and could see my son's heartbeat jump on the screen.

Everything appeared to be fine, until Elizabeth began to wince in pain. She was holding her head, and before I even had a chance to ask her what was wrong, her eyes closed, and her doctor arrived screaming for assistance. "Code Blue in room 5146B, Code Blue."

I began screaming at the doctor, "What's wrong with my wife?" I was ignored, and they began to work on Elizabeth. I was literally pushed out of the room as I watched my wife fight for two lives: her own and our son's. What the hell just happened? We were laughing and talking, and now she has a team of doctors surrounding her.

I felt powerless. No one would tell me anything. Hospital staff was entering and exiting her room, machines were brought in. *Someone tell me what the hell is going on?*

I fell to the floor and held my head between my knees. I never prayed so hard in my life. "Please God, don't take my family away from me. Please watch over them." My tears began to fall when her doctor and a man I never met approached me. I shakily rose from the floor and was asked to join them in another room where it was more private. I demanded to know what the hell was happening with my wife, but they insisted we move to a room where we can be alone. I had no choice but to follow.

"Mr. Reed, this is Dr. Leviatian, he is our head of Neurology Department here at Cedars-Sinai."

"Hello. What's wrong with my wife? And why does she need a Neurologist?"

"Mr. Reed, I'm very sorry, but your wife suffered a Hemorrhagic Stroke. It's what we call Arteriovenous Malformations (AVMs). It is a congenital malformation of blood vessels in the brain that can rupture into the brain tissue as they get larger. In your wife's individual case, they may have been increased in size due to her pregnancy."

"What are you telling me? My wife, Elizabeth… she's dead?" as soon as the words left my mouth, I reached for a wastebasket and vomited profusely until nothing was left. I felt all my strength leave my body as the two doctors helped me back into my chair.

"Mr. Reed, your wife is on a respirator keeping her and your child alive right now. Technically your wife has been declared brain dead. She will never wake up. Time is of the essence, she is being prepped right now for an emergency C-Section. If your child has any chance of survival, we must take him now. We just need your consent."

My instinct to protect my child gave me the strength to move. We quickly arrived at the OR where I saw Elizabeth strapped to the table. I held her hand and listened to the whooshing sound of the monitor keeping her alive.

"SIR, I'M SORRY to disturb you, but your son needs to be fed." The sweet grey haired nurse had returned, bringing me out of my tortured memories of the night's events.

"Can I feed him," I asked.

"Why don't you let me do it for now? Dr. Leviatian and his team would like to speak with you." *Of course they do. They want to rip out my Elizabeth's organs, and completely ravage her beautiful body.*

I could feel the walls of my chest tightening around my heart. I was in so much pain and at the same time, so in love with my child. "Please be careful with him, he's all I have left of my wife," I say as I gently lay a kiss on his delicate head.

"I will, sir, and I'm so very sorry for your loss." Somehow her words gave me comfort. She reminded me of Lila, Reese's grandmother. I made my way down the long corridor, and that's when I heard angered voices.

"This is my hell, Phillip. God is punishing me for what I did to Walker. He has taken my precious daughter away from me. Sins of the father. My sins. Your sins. They have led us here to this moment," Henry cries out in pain.

"Pull yourself together, man. No one could predict what happened to Elizabeth. It was an unforeseen tragedy, and you have to stop this crazy talk right now. Walker has been through enough, he can't handle you breaking down too. We made our choices, Henry. Now live with them, as I have had to."

"What the hell is going on here?" I burst through the door. I only made out a few words from their conversation, but I knew I had heard my name.

"There you are, son. We were worried about you. Can we get anything for you?" my father appeared to be all too eager to change the subject. While my father paced the hallway, Henry took me in his arms.

"I am so sorry." He weeps again on my shoulder. I have cried enough of my own tears to last me a lifetime. He asks, "What happens now?"

"I have to meet with the transplant team now. They are going to let us say our goodbyes before taking Elizabeth. Where's Gail? She needs to be here."

"Oh dear god, my baby girl. Why did this happen to her?" He takes me in his arms, and he breaks down once again. I don't know how much more I can take, but my father seems to read me like a book and helps me detach from Elizabeth's distraught father. I silently thank him.

After talking with the doctors and transplant team, I signed the papers. I wanted to be the last one to say goodbye to Elizabeth, so I waited outside for her parents and my parents to finish. It felt like an eternity, but they needed their closure. How can any of us ever have closure to this tragedy? Yesterday I had everything a man could want in one's lifetime. Now in the next few days, I will be placing my beautiful wife in the cold ground. How is that fair? Why my wife?

Our son had been brought to me as our families were exiting her room. I realized not one of them has even had a chance to really look at him or even hold him. I didn't want to let him go, but they had every right to meet their grandchild.

"Oh my goodness, he is so beautiful. He has her eyes. Henry, come look at your grandson." Gail's tears stopped falling and were replaced with smiles. Elizabeth was living on through our son. He would be the one to heal all of us.

"Have you decided on a name for your boy, son?" My father is probably thinking he will be named after him.

"Yes, we named him the minute we found out he was a boy. Please meet Jackson Walker Reed." Their eyes lit up, and our mothers began to cry again. Phillip just patted me on my back, while Henry began to fall apart again. I could take no more, and I excused myself. I needed my time with Elizabeth. I carried Jackson in my arms, and sat beside Elizabeth. She looked so peaceful, a sleeping angel. I knew she was gone, but her heart was still beating, and I wanted our son to feel his mother. I placed him gently beside her and held him in place as I began telling him about his beautiful mother.

"Jackson, this is your mommy, Elizabeth. She loves you so much. She will always be with you my son. For the rest of your life, you will carry your mother in your heart, as she watches over you from the heavens above. Never be afraid, she is the strongest person I know, and not a day will go by that you won't feel her love running through you. She taught me so much, and even when I was facing my darkest hours, she was there to bring me back to life."

"Your mother saved me, and gave me the greatest treasure I will ever receive. She gave me you, Jackson. I love you so much, and I promise you that I will never fail you. You are my life, and you will always have me on your side."

Our son cooed with hearing my words, he is only hours old, but I know he recognizes my voice. I talked to Elizabeth's belly every single day and night. We sang to him, read stories, and every time we had finished, he would kick his mother. I guess he liked what he was hearing.

My time was up. With Elizabeth attached to a machine, I couldn't take a picture of them, so I just mentally stored the image of my son in his mother's embrace. It would forever be in my memory. I would relive this moment with Jackson when he was ready to hear it. The transplant team was waiting up in the OR for my wife. I placed Jackson back in his rolling bassinet and kissed my wife one last time.

"I love you, Elizabeth. Thank you for our life together. Thank you for our son. I will not fail you or him. Please watch over us, I never thought I would be doing this without you. I'm going to need your strength to guide me and show me the way. I know your confidence in me, but I'm still scared. God! I'm going to miss you." I wept and tried to hold her the best I could. I didn't want to let her go. This was hell. How can this be happening? I was lost in my grief when the transplant team had arrived. I was oblivious to their presence.

"I'm sorry, sir, but its time." I nodded and stepped aside so the team could move her.

I HELD MY son once more, as I watched Elizabeth be taken away by the team of doctors. She would be responsible for saving lives today, while hers was lost.

THE END…FOR NOW

THE FOREVER SERIES CONTINUES WITH WALKER AND REESE'S STORY IN BOOK TWO, **SECOND CHANCE AT FOREVER** SCHEDULED FOR RELEASE IN AUGUST, 2014.

BONUS SURPRISE

We meet again…

What would you do if given a second chance to right a wrong from your past… A wrong that should have never happened… A wrong that haunts you every day…

Would you stop at nothing to reclaim the one person you built your entire future around? **Hell, Yes!…You would!**

Walker Reed, has everything a man could desire.

Power…Success…Wealth…

What he didn't have was Reese Mitchell. The one woman who held his heart. One night she walked out of his life; disappearing without a trace, shattering Walker, and causing his heart to ache for her return.

Seventeen years later…fate has reunited them with an unexpected twist. His **Second Chance at Forever** is standing before him and looking as beautiful as he remembers her to be.

Determined to find out why she left him, Walker will not stop to learn the truth.

He's taking back what's his…This time around, he will not let her go…

ACKNOWLEDGMENTS

First and foremost a big thank you to **Kathleen.** You wore many hats helping me bring this book to life. Thank you so much for our talks, the laughter you always bring, and the smiles that I carry with me. You bring so much to my writing and make me better. Your support and encouragement means so much. I will forever be thankful for the universe bringing us together in friendship. XO

Trudie: Thank you for being my number one beta reader. I'm never nervous when I send you something to read for me. I love your comments and your creative feedback. You make me laugh out loud with your excitement. Thank you for joining me on this crazy ride I call my life. Sisters Forever!

Richard: You inspire me in so many ways. Wine night would not be possible without you. Ti amo il mio amico.

Joe: My newest member of my reading team, but always my friend first. Thank you for your friendship and what it brings to our family.

To my readers: Thank you for joining me on this journey of mine, for loving my characters, and for all the love and support you show me. I read every single message left for me on my Facebook author page. It warms my heart to know that something that I have created makes you all smile.

For my beautiful friend from Italy: Ad Angela, grazie per la tua amicizia e per il support al mio lavoro. E stato un onore conoscere te e la tua bella famiglia. Un ricordo che conservero sempre. Ti am oil mio amico.

Thank you: Sarah Hansen of Okay Creations. Once again you designed an amazing cover for me. They are proudly lining the walls of my home.

Julie Titus of JT Formatting. Your unique style and creative imagination brings my book to life…page by page. Thank you for all that you do.

Natalie Catalano of Love Between the Sheets. Thank you for all of your hard work organizing my blog tours. Thank you for introducing my work to all of the bloggers who gave me a read and review. It means so much to be accepted, and I am so grateful for all of you.

ABOUT THE AUTHOR

I call New Jersey my home where I live and share my life with my husband, Henry, and our three sons. Every day is a busy one around the Wasowski home. We all seem to be running in many directions, but at the end of the day we come together as one.

To write my first book was an accomplishment I never thought would be realized. I remember on release day for "A Changed Life" my best friend kept telling me this: "Be happy, Mary, you wrote a book!" My friend was right. I am beyond happy and so very blessed. I have met amazing people along the way, and I am fortunate enough to call them my friends. We are a sisterhood doing what we love, and sharing our words with all of you.

I was and still am a devoted reader and fan of Adult Contemporary Romance Novels. I love to spend time with a good book and get lost in the story. I am a huge re-reader of my favorites. I do hope my book "Forever" touches your heart. Walker and Reese are a strong couple with many struggles to overcome on their path to their happily ever after. I hope you continue to read their story as it will continue in "Second Chance at Forever" and conclude with "Our Forever Promise."

I would love to hear from you. Please feel free to reach out to me:

Email: authormaryawasowski@gmail.com

Website: http://authormaryawasowski.com/

Facebook: https://www.facebook.com/home.php#!/pages/Author-Mary-A-Wasowski/332971356804341

Twitter: https://twitter.com/wasow6